THE SAVANNAH GONDOLIER

THE SAINTS OF SAVANNAH SERIES

LEIGH EBBERWEIN

Sister Pat,
Thank you for your support. Happy Reading!
Much love,
Leigh Ebberwein

Old Fort Press
Savannah, Georgia

ISBN: 978-1-7376152-4-8 (Paperback)

ISBN: 978-1-7376152-3-1 (E-book)

Old Fort Press
Savannah, Georgia

CONTENTS

"SONG FOR LAZARETTO"

For years, when ships reached Tybee Light,
they'd stop at South Channel Sound.
They'd unload the sick and the dying,
both the free, ... and the bound.
They'd leave them here, where this little
    creek,
still far from Savannah town,
touches the back of the island
on the side where the sun goes down ...
at a place called 'lazaretto,'
where a quarantine would hold
all the ones with dreaded diseases,
and the ones too sick to be sold.

— CYNTHIA FARR KINKEL

1

EBB AND FLOW

Savannah Beach, Tybee Island, Georgia

There are those who are born near the ocean and set their clocks to the hour of the tides. They come and go like the gentle flow of the current as it ebbs and flows and are happiest when they are near salt water. Maggie was one of those people.

A small sigh escaped her mouth as Maggie drank in her surroundings. It was the most beautiful time of day in a shrimper's life, the moment when the pitch black of night meets the orange brink of day. The rest of the world had no idea what they were missing each morning when the sun unfolded across the water. Maybe they were the lucky ones because they were not drawn to the ocean; however, she couldn't imagine her life without those moments.

Maggie watched the Tybee lighthouse come into view as her dad turned the shrimp boat towards Lazaretto Creek, heading back in. "Why does this perfect summer have to end?"

"All good things must come to an end," her dad answered.

She nodded but still questioned why. Maggie would begin her first day of high school that morning and had convinced her dad to take her on one last morning run before this dreadful school year began. Maggie had gone to Catholic school her whole life, but Trevor had been there. They had been friends for as long as she could remember. But now, she would be going to a place where he could not follow, the all-girls Catholic high school in Savannah.

As the boat approached the dock, she could see the headlights of her mom's car up on the bluff, waiting to take her to school and away from her beloved water. She rolled her eyes as she jumped from the boat to the dock. All she wanted was to be on the water; going to school was a waste of time. But what choice did she have? She pulled the green-plaid uniform skirt over her gym shorts and sulked to the car.

Maggie had no way of knowing this perfect morning would unfold into a life-changing day. Today she would learn the excitement life offered between the beauty of sunrise and the serenity of sunset. It was the people in the middle that mattered. Today was the day she would meet her tribe.

2

THE POKER GAME

13 Years Later

Alex and James met the first and third Tuesday of every month for poker. They had a standing reservation for the back room at The Brass Rail, a favorite Tybee bar. They had picked up three other friends: Harold, who owned the bar; Richard; who owned Tybee Motors; and Arthur, Tybee's ex-mayor. Everyone would bring extra money, always beginning with a full glass of bourbon and a handful of cigars. It was a table-stakes game. Lighthearted and fun, the group always celebrated the evening winner by making him buy the last round. That was, until one particular evening.

James arrived late. Savannah had been hit by a five-day weather system that brought forty-knot winds and ten-foot swells. He was tired from being awake the night before and knocked around on the water for days. He grunted when he sat down, "I'm getting too old for this shit. My body doesn't take a beating like it once did."

Alex joked with him, just like he always did. "That cushy little job of yours. Try being knocked around on a shrimp boat, tossed around like a rag doll, then pulling in empty nets. At least you're steady on those big ships."

"Yeah, once I'm on them. But you try and make the jump from the pilot boat crashing against a car carrier with those waves and climbing a pilot ladder in heavy winds. I've kept my rosary beads near me all week long."

"That's what you get paid the big bucks for," Alex answered, half kidding.

The two men always teased one another. Both working on the river, they had great respect for each other. But something about Alex's statement rubbed James the wrong way that night. Staring Alex down, he said, "Some of us don't have the luxury of working when we feel like it. We don't have a spouse paying the bills."

"Are you saying I'm slack and let Victoria support the family?"

"Take it as you will, but you should be happy to know that Maggie will be well taken care of by the "big bucks," as you call it, once she and Trevor marry.

"My little girl doesn't need to be taken care of. She can stand on her own two feet just fine," Alex replied as he watched the final hand being dealt.

The last game was five-card draw. Alex's eyes lit up when he saw his hand and quickly opened for $100. The other men grumbled, but all put in, just to get their other cards. Both Alex and James drew just one card.

Alex said, "I'll bet $300." It was everything he had.

The other men folded, except for James. He studied his cards for a while and said, "I'll raise $500."

Alex looked to the table, knowing his till was empty. He glanced at James and wanted to punch the smug grin right off his face. He took a deep breath, questioning what he was about to do, but continued, "I'll wager my shrimp boat, *The Victoria*." The room went silent as the group looked to James to answer.

James thumped the edge of his cards with his thumb. He opened his mouth to speak but closed it quickly. Running his hand across his face, he murmured, "I'll wager Lazaretto River Sports."

Alex eyed him warily, "That's not yours to wager."

"Actually, it is. As of last week."

Alex thought for a moment, then nodded, so James called the hand. Alex slowly set down a ten, jack, queen, king, and ace of hearts - a straight flush. James' face reddened as he slung his four sevens across the table and stood up so fast his chair fell to the floor. Leaning on the table, he narrowed his eyes at Alex. "You have tortured me for thirty years, and I'm done. I wipe my hands of you, Victoria, and," he paused but then continued, "and Maggie. I break all ties and assure you that my son, Trevor, will too." Then he grabbed his jacket and walked out into the pouring rain.

He sat in his BMW, staring at the door he had just stormed out of. *Why am I so angry? Why now, after all this time?* he wondered. Alex and James had been friends since they were young boys. They had spent their summers together on Tybee and knew every inch of the island, from its sandy beach to its muddy rivers. Although they had been born into very different worlds, they had been poured from the same mold and complemented each other well. When they were younger, they loved to play chase along the shore. As they grew older, the only things they chased were girls. Subsequently, they both fell for the same one, Victoria.

Every year, James' family had moved from their Washington Avenue white Tudor house to their airy beach cottage that was anything but a cottage. The house sat high on Officers Row overlooking the shipping channel. It was a beautiful old house with floor-to-ceiling windows, hardwood floors, a wraparound porch, and a grand dining room where they held many parties.

Alex and Victoria's families had never been on the invitation list. They were what some called "Tybee Trash," but James never saw it that way. He loved being with them. They were exciting and fun and could do things he was never allowed to do. He was captivated by their carefree lifestyle. James' path in life had been set the day his mother had delivered her first child, a boy. He was the first son of a River Pilot, a coveted and respected job along any port city, and the honor would be passed down to him.

But like all good things, this job came with a price. The day after he graduated from high school, he began the grueling apprenticeship with an uncertain completion date. He would be required to dedicate his life, day and night, to the Savannah River. That dedication left very little time for family and friends, and eventually, his relationship with both Alex and Victoria changed.

In his absence, Alex and Victoria's relationship thrived, and they were soon married. Losing Victoria was the only regret James had about becoming a river pilot. In his heart, he had somehow pictured the two of them, married with children. That image haunted him, even after thirty years. He didn't see Victoria nearly as much as he would have liked. She stayed busy working at the hospital. However, he still enjoyed his time with Alex. Just like in their youth, they balanced each other well. As a bonus, he had been able to keep up with Victoria's life.

But that bonus had come with a price. Years of wanting another man's wife had finally infringed on his sanity; his mind couldn't take it. However, his jealousy wasn't the main reason he felt unbalanced; it was the bad dreams. They had begun the night he had been given the property on Lazaretto Creek. He prayed that losing the land in the poker game would take them away.

MAGGIE AWOKE to the sound of banging. Struggling to open her eyes, she noticed the light from early dawn barely shining through the blinds. She flipped on light switches as she stumbled to the front door almost frantically. Nothing good could have happened during the night to be awakened at this time of the morning. Her heart raced as she opened the door to Trevor.

She had seen many faces of Trevor over the last six years and knew them all by heart. But the one he was wearing today was new, and it frightened her. "What's wrong? What happened?" she asked, holding her breath until he spoke.

"I can't see you anymore," he spit out coldly.

"You can't see me? What does that even mean?" She stepped back and narrowed her eyes to examine him. What had happened? They had gone to dinner the night before, and everything was perfect. In fact, it was beyond perfect. They had discussed where they would live once his apprenticeship was complete. How could he have changed his mind so quickly? His eyes were bloodshot, but not from drinking. He had been crying. "Come inside. We need to talk about this..."

He cut her off. "There's nothing to talk about. Goodbye, Maggie." He jumped into his truck and drove off without looking back.

Maggie stood in the doorway. "What. Just. Happened?" she muttered aloud. She stumbled out to the one and only step of her Tybee ranch-style house and sat down. Burying her head in her hands, she muttered, "What in the hell just happened?"

Closing her eyes, she replayed the last several weeks of their relationship. Trevor spent most of his time on the river, either on a ship or at the pilot base. He was usually distracted or tired when she did see him, constantly worrying about when the next ship would arrive or depart the large port. He was always connected to his office and seldom had time to relax or even sleep. But this was the life they had chosen, and they had chosen it together. She knew what she was getting into when they started dating.

They had been friends since birth. She had watched how his family operated with crazy schedules and his dad's absence from many events. She reasoned she was a strong woman and could hold down the fort in his absence. But the bottom line was she loved him. She would treasure every minute she had with him.

She tried to choke back the cry in her throat, but it

seeped out, loud and ugly. She barely heard the sound of gravel crunching down the street until it was almost in front of her house. Hope filled her heart. *He's coming back*, she thought as she looked up, but was disappointed to see her dad's old pickup pulling into the drive. *"Oh great! He never visits, and he chooses today? Two visits before seven a.m. How could I be so lucky?"* She took a deep breath and wiped her face with the sleeve of her pajama top.

Alex spotted Maggie sitting on the step and approached her with worry on his face. "What's the matter, baby girl?" he asked his only child. That's when she broke out crying again. He quickly sat beside her on the stair and wrapped her in his arms.

She tried to talk in between sobs. "Trevor just dumped me, and I have no idea why. He won't even talk to me. What am I gonna do, Daddy?"

Her dad held her tight. He knew the reason his daughter's heart was broken, and he knew he was to blame. He would tell her; she deserved to know. But just not yet. He would help her get through this, then tell her once the dust settled.

3

HONOR

For centuries, the canals of Venice were the lifeforce of the great city. Just like the veins of a savage beast, the canals pulsed life through its body of 120 islands and the 435 bridges connecting them. Many types of watercraft constantly moved through the waterways and the neighboring lagoon, shuttling residents and visitors to their many destinations.

The water gave Venetians protection, and the men who captained these vessels were held in high regard. Like the mythical ferryman steering across the River Styx, these men worked day and night carrying people to their destinations. The most mysterious of all were the gondoliers.

There were several upper-class families in Venice, but the Biancos were at the top. Their ancestors were ancient Venetian nobility, so they still enjoyed a high social position and owned a good portion of Venice's businesses. For hundreds of years, the Vianello family had been the private gondoliers for the Biancos. It was a local honor to be at the family's disposal. The gondolier was awarded an unprecedented salary and the privilege to commandeer the most elegant gondola in Venice.

There was a line of succession that was followed when choosing the premiere gondolier; the position and rules had been put in place for centuries and the Biancos made no exceptions. The honor was bestowed to the first born son of the current gondolier. If there was no son, or if that son hadn't passed the test of the gondolier, the position would go back to the original line and pass to the second son. That was the case for Claudio.

THE STORM ENGULFED the boat in a matter of minutes as Claudio rowed hard, searching for safety. He was in a long stretch of the canal, which lacked mooring poles to tie the boat up to; still he scanned his surroundings, praying for an answer. If he got too close to the palazzo walls, the wind would knock his boat and its passengers hard against it. His best bet was to position the boat in the center of the channel, away from everyone else.

That morning had started like every other. Claudio was to retrieve a foreign dignitary and his family from their luxury hotel, which sat on a neighboring canal, and to bring them to Bianco Enterprises. He had been employed by the Biancos for twenty-five years, but it seemed like an eternity.

He could hardly remember his carefree days of waiting in line to ferry a tourist on a cheery ride through Venice. His days were now filled watching the clock to get businessmen and dignitaries to appointments.

As he approached the hotel's entrance, he heard the patter of a drumming sound. He ran his eyes along the dock until finding its source, the wife. She was tapping her heeled shoes impatiently. Once he made eye contact with the testy woman, the tapping increased until his gondola was secure, and he held out his hand to help her on board. The husband stepped in behind her, leaving their fourteen-year-old son standing on the dock.

The boy bounced up and down in excitement. Although he was a teenager and appeared to be about the same size as Claudio, his face and actions were comparable to a young boy. When Claudio asked him if he wanted to go on a boat ride, the boy squealed with excitement but then looked down worriedly at the water.

"You'll be safe," Claudio reassured him. "I promise." The boy reached out to him and settled in the seat facing the rear. *The trust of a child*, Claudio thought. As they pushed off, the frightened boy began to whimper. The couple stared straight ahead, as if waiting for someone else to handle their nervous child. Most of the dignitaries Claudio shuttled around Venice seemed preoccupied and selfish. He wondered why he continued to work this job.

The job had been thrust upon Claudio when his older brother, Alvise, who was only 45, died in his sleep. His son, Pietro, was next in line for the position. However, Pietro had not completed his training. Claudio offered to train Pietro, in order to qualify him for the position, but Mr. Bianco wouldn't make an exception.

Mr. Bianco had explained to Claudio, "There are rules that must be followed. You are the next in line for this position. You are the only Vianello whose credentials are in place. I understand if you do not wish to accept the position, but if that's the case, it will be passed from the Vianello family for the unforeseeable future."

Claudio knew that his family's honor was at stake. "That can never happen. It would be an honor, sir." The two men had become close friends, and the Vianello family name stayed strong. However, now that he was nearing sixty, he was getting tired. Maybe the time had come to retire.

As each cloud continued to roll upon them, a veil of fear crept further upon the boy's face. Claudio wished there was something he could do to ease his worries and regretted the promise he had made to protect him. He rowed hard, so hard his arms began to cramp. When Claudio looked up, the boy was staring right in his face, terrified. Claudio tried to smile, but it physically hurt the muscles in his face due to the tension in his body.

The husband and wife spewed their frustrations, as if Claudio had summoned the storm by his own hand. They watched the wall of rain coming down the canal, found a throw blanket stashed under the seat, and pulled it over their heads in preparation. As the storm drew near, the boy stood straight up, looking side to side for where to flee.

When the rain finally was upon them, it came down hard. The downpour created a sensation of needles upon Claudio's skin. The boy screamed, swatting at his arms as if being stung by a swarm of bees. His movement caused the boat to list. Claudio froze, hoping to balance the gondola from the back, while the boy's parents still paid their son no attention. The thunder let out a deafening boom at the exact moment the boy hit the murky water as if the storm was claiming the boy for its own. Claudio yelled out to the couple, who only stared at the spot on the water that had swallowed their boy.

The boy didn't resurface. As each second passed, Claudio realized the boy's life was in danger and he was the only one who would try to save him. Releasing his fórcola, he dove in. He grabbed the boy's flailing arm; the boy grasped Claudio in a death grip. They sank further and further towards the canal's bottom until Claudio pinched the boy hard to release his grip and maneuvered the boy quickly to the surface.

The couple screamed as Claudio and the boy broke through the water. The foreigner leaned over to pull the boy inside the vessel, but struggled with his weight. Claudio pushed his backside from the water, and together they succeeded in getting the child into the gondola.

Claudio trod water, wondering how far the boat had drifted while he had been submerged. That's when the large vaporetto water bus struck, crushing him between the two vessels. He slowly prayed the Act of Contrition. His last thoughts were of Rosa and his children, as his world went black forever.

Michael Vianello witnessed the entire accident and rushed over in his gondola to help, but it had been too late. A film of blood laid upon the surface of the water as everyone watched him pull Claudio onto his boat. Many boats bobbed around in the storm, but no one offered to help. The man's eyes were fully open, staring into the great abyss of nothingness. The same eyes that held so much kindness for everyone around him now had no life left in them. Michael tried to look away from them but couldn't, so he ran his finger down the man's face and shut his eyes forever.

4

DISGRACE

Venice, Italy

Michael stumbled in the front door of his home and stood motionless in the foyer. Finally alone, he felt the cry crawl into his throat. He had never seen someone die before; he couldn't get the image out of his mind. He didn't hear his mother's heels clipping towards the door.

Monica stood back from Michael in horror, pointing to his blood-stained black and white gondola shirt. "Where are you hurt?" she shrieked, over and over again. The pitch of her voice hurt his ears. He needed quiet and lacked the energy to comfort someone else.

"It's not my blood, Mom," was all he said as he pulled off his shirt and walked to the kitchen. He threw the shirt into the trash, hoping to discard the horrible memory it held. He would never be able to unsee those dead eyes looking at him. He ran his head under the large porcelain sink, trying to wash away traces of the blood he kept visualizing but were no longer there.

As he wiped his face with the kitchen towel, he searched for the words to describe what he had just witnessed and slowly began. "I was on the Grand Canal running my regular route when a terrible storm came out of nowhere. Some of us were lucky enough to secure our boats before it hit, but others were not." His voice cracked, and he paused. "Papa's uncle Claudio was safe in the center of the channel until a boy he was ferrying fell overboard. When he dove in to save him, his gondola drifted into the vaporetto lane." He was so choked up that he could barely finish the sentence. He cleared his throat and spit out, "Claudio was struck from behind and died instantly."

Michael slid into a kitchen chair and rubbed his hand across his face. The sadness of holding a man who had just left this world was too much to comprehend; his thoughts went directly to his own father. What if it had been his dad? His mother sat next to him and placed her hand on his back. She rarely touched him, even as a child. The warmth of her touch broke him, and he began to cry. His dad was the one to always comfort him. He felt his mom grow tense. She gave Michael two quick pats on his back, stood up, and poured him a glass of water.

Sitting back down, she began to question Michael. "Your father's Uncle Claudio got hit by the vaporetto? Claudio Vianello?"

"Yes, Mama."

"And did several people witness the whole thing?"

"No, Mama. Just me."

Monica stood from the table and walked into the dining

room. Leaning against the wall, she took a slow intake of air and tried to clear her head. She had waited for this moment for so long, and now it had been given to her. And by her son, no less. What were the odds of that?

Her thoughts flashed back to a scene 25 years ago, the morning when all of her dreams had been snatched from her. She remembered the written promise given to her husband by Mr. Bianco's assistant, Sergio. She had stored it safely in a small box that was both fireproof and waterproof and had placed it inside her china cabinet. After pulling it out, she read the words once again. *If any hardship or disgrace ever comes upon our next gondolier, the family of Pietro Vianello will be our immediate choice.* She placed it back in the box, then slowly walked back into the kitchen and sat in the chair next to Michael.

"Have you spoken to anyone since the accident?" she asked.

"No," he replied. "Everyone was busy trying to get the family off the gondola, clean up the mess, and calm the people on the vaporetto. They asked me to wait a couple of hours before coming in to give my statement."

She stared at Michael intently, then began, "I'm sorry you witnessed such a tragedy. It was a shame Uncle Claudio was in the wrong place in the channel. The rain must have confused him."

Michael disputed, "But he wasn't in the wrong place at all. He had drifted trying to save the boy."

She kept her voice steady but firm, "You couldn't see well in the rain either. Claudio was in the vaporetto lane."

Michael raised his voice, "No, Mama, he did everything right; he died a hero."

"He died, God bless his soul, and God bless his family, but you must tell the truth that he was in the wrong," she demanded.

Michael had no energy to fight with his mom, so he sat quietly. Then he began to put together what she was saying. He remembered his mom explaining that if any shame or wrongdoing came to Claudio, his dad would regain the honor he should have been given. He gave his mom a questioning look, and she continued, "Claudio was a good man, and he saved that boy. It was a shame he was in the wrong place when it happened, right?"

Michael slowly shook his head no.

Monica asked a little more sternly, "Right?" and she stared into Michael's eyes, boring into his battered soul until he slowly closed his eyes and nodded his head, yes.

"Something good *can* come from this tragedy," was all she said. Michael listened to the click of her heels as she walked out of the kitchen, down the hall, and out the front door.

5

THE HEALERS OF TORCELLO

A slow smile spread across Monica's face as she quickly made her way to the flower shop. She felt a twinge of guilt for placing a drop of her medicine into Michael's water, but she knew him too well. It would be difficult for him to tell a lie. Her treatment, as she referred to her concoction, would help him do what needed to be done.

Monica was about to burst and knew she must tell someone her news, so she called Mita into the shop's backroom and began to tell the story of the accident. As the account ended, a small tear trickled down Mita's face. She was so sensitive. "Poor Claudio," Mita whispered, shaking her head. "Another Vianello is gone. So sad. And poor Michael. How is he?"

"He's fine," Monica answered, knowing that a small lie would end the conversation. How could Mita care so much? She hardly ever saw Pietro or Michael, but the woman still felt a strong connection to both of them. It was the bond of family, especially large families.

Monica left quickly; she never stayed long. Mita wondered why she had come at all. She seemed happy delivering bad news about her family. Mita would never understand how Monica wasn't satisfied with her wonderful life. She would give anything to have the love of a man like Pietro and a wonderful son like Michael. But Monica had always wanted more.

She thought back to when Monica first moved to Venice. She had shown up at the flower shop holding a small overnight bag in one hand and a plant in the other. Mita knew the plant well, the mandrake. She also knew what it could do, both the good and the bad. She was surprised her family had entrusted a fifteen-year-old with such a powerful weapon and decided to give her younger cousin one of the empty rooms in the back of the shop to store it. Then she had taken Monica up the back stairway and into the two-bedroom apartment above the shop.

"How is the family and the Clarise Sisters?" Mita asked.

"The same. Exactly the same as when you left," was her simple reply.

"Well, I'll leave you to get settled. Let me know if you have any questions," Mita called over her shoulder as she walked back to the shop. She had known things would be difficult but could not predict what was to come.

Mita had been the first child from the family who had been allowed to leave Torcello. Following in the footsteps of the Clarisse nuns who she had served beside, she felt called to become one herself. She was sent to Venice to discern that call. After two years of formation, she couldn't make the lifetime commitment to religious life, but felt a deep connection to helping the people of Venice in their everyday life. Her family in Torcello liked having someone inside the mother city and decided to let her stay if she could find a way to support herself. The flower shop, with a small two-bedroom flat above, was the perfect answer.

Her parents had sent word that Monica was coming. They didn't ask; they never did. For generations, the family worked hand-in-hand with the order of Clarisse nuns. The nuns lived a life of poverty and served the people on the neighboring islands. They called upon her family frequently. The good sisters combined their power of prayer with the healer's knowledge of the land to keep the people well. And so, it had continued for centuries.

Monica had wanted more. At an early age, people began to notice her gifts. She was good with concoctions and seemed to know what to apply for specific ailments. As she entered her teen years, her curiosity clouded her abilities. Her parents were bewildered by her unquenchable desire to leave the island. They decided it might be better to let her go for a short time; perhaps she would get it out of her system. So, they made arrangements for Monica to stay with Mita.

Monica had fallen in love with the city. She treated Mita as a hostess instead of family and made no attempts to get to know any more about her. What Monica's parents hoped she would overcome became almost an obsession. She wanted more of what life had to offer and drank deeply of the Venetian culture.

Mita had watched closely as Monica's abilities flourished. Although the two women shared a great knowledge of plants, Mita used her abilities to help others. She kept an eye on the selfishness of the teenage girl and prayed that the good that lay inside of Monica would overcome the bad. She had great hopes she and Monica could run the flower shop together; they could help so many people. But that hope soon disappeared.

Monica worked hard at the flower shop during the day, but most nights she could be found in its backroom meeting with people who pleaded for her help. She learned from the people of Venice: what motivated them, what annoyed them, and their secret desires. Soon people sought her out, asking for remedies for anything from anxiety to a potion for love.

Monica blossomed into a beautiful woman, something Mita had never done. Before long, she had a string of suitors begging for her hand. However, Monica knew that her family wouldn't let her stay in Venice indefinitely. They would pull her back when needed, and her time was running out quickly. So, she found the perfect anchor to the city she loved. She married a Venetian whose job held him to the island. Pietro had been her ideal shield.

Once married, she left working at the flower shop to begin her perfect life. However, she kept the room in the back. Over time, Mita became suspicious about Monica's clientele. She also noticed that the original mandrake plant wasn't growing; it was being used little by little. Soon it would all be gone. So Mita watched silently. She watched and kept detailed notes.

6

DOLPHIN

Venice, Italy

L eo climbed into the boat and lowered the motor. He had never been so ready to get away from the sneers and rude comments that surrounded him. It was hard to believe that a job that once brought him so much joy now only brought sorrow. He wasn't sure how much longer he could endure it.

As he slowly made his way out of the canal, he noticed his pain decrease as his distance from Venice increased. He inhaled a deep breath as he hit open water. The scent of the lagoon gave him the peace he needed; he acknowledged it with a reverent bow of his head and a small smile. His mom would often tell him saltwater ran through his veins and frequently told the story of his birth. She had delivered him on the floor of his papa's gondola while trying to make it to the nearby San Giovanni e Paolo Hospital with its emergency entrance on the canal. Subsequently, the gentle pull of the water had been his compass ever since.

Passing Murano, he slowed his boat, then moved at idle speed as he made way towards Sant' Erasmus Island. When the island came into view, he cut the engine and drifted. The sunset was an explosion of orange and pinks. "Pink skies at night, sailors delight," he said under his breath. That's when he heard it. He sat up, looked around, and saw the threads of water rippling. The top of their heads glided into view, followed by their dorsal fins bowing back into the water: dolphins. Several people had claimed to see them, but there had never been dolphins around Venice, so their presence had been a surprise.

He grinned and thought back to that summer in Savannah when he was a boy and of the many dolphins that swam in the creeks around Tybee Island. Then he remembered the girl, Maggie. She would beat on the side of her boat, and the dolphins would come, just like puppies running for a treat. He leaned over the side of his boat and started knocking. Sure enough, the dolphins popped right up out of the water. Looking around the boat, he found some bait his brother had left in the well from the night before and threw it over to the family of four. They circled and even buoyed out of the water to look inside the boat. Once the fish were gone, so were the dolphin.

His thoughts went back to Savannah and running the streets with Maggie, who spent the summer with her grandmother. The house was next to his aunt and uncle; now, it was just his aunt. When Leo's dad had traveled to Savannah for his uncle's funeral two years ago, he had come home with many stories about Maggie. She had inherited her grandmother's house and had kept a watchful eye on his aunt and uncle. His dad had caught up with her on that visit and found it funny that a woman would own an adventure kayaking company. But Leo had to admit that it had intrigued him.

As his boat moved along slowly with the tide, he continued to think of Maggie. A slow smile spread across his face as he formulated a plan in his head. As night set upon him, he started his engine and headed home.

Leo kissed his mom's forehead as he walked onto the patio, wishing he could take her sadness away. She grabbed his hand as it lay upon her shoulder and gently patted it. Every evening she retreated to the same spot on the side of the house; the same spot she and his father had spent every afternoon. As children, they had known it was their parent's private time together and had been trained not to interrupt, but now she sat alone.

Over the last year, since his father's death, Leo would come home from work and enter from the side of the house, where he could see his mom. For hundreds of years, her family had made their living on Sant' Erasmus Island, providing vegetables for all of Venice. She, and his three siblings, continued the practice and harvested the tastiest produce that was now shipped to many parts of the Veneto region. Her days were jam-packed, so there was little time to grieve, but her nights were filled with sorrow.

Rosa turned to look her oldest child in the eyes. "How was your day?"

"The same, Mama. People still talk. I can't believe that someone from our family started this. Why does Michael hate us so?"

"Your father and his brother, Alvise, were far apart in age. That made it hard for the two of them to be close, but they did try. However, when Alvise passed away," she paused and made the Sign of the Cross, "his son Pietro wasn't a licensed gondolier. Your father was asked to take the position. Pietro and his hateful wife haven't spoken to us since. Claudio said that Pietro's son, Michael, was a nice boy but I think he was caught in the crossfire and follows what his parents tell him." She stopped and took Leo's face into her hands and gave him a weak smile, "You miss your papa; I understand."

"Yes, very much. The stories they tell about the accident rarely hold any truth. And no-one ever mentions the boy he saved." He let his eyes fall to the empty chair where his father once sat. "I'm thinking of taking some time to go see Aunt Regina in Savannah. Papa worried about her after her husband's death. I will call her tomorrow."

Rosa nodded, understanding the many reasons Leo was leaving. "I think that would be a great idea," she said as she kissed the side of his face while gently making the Sign of the Cross with her thumb on his forehead. Rosa watched Leo walk under the trellis that hung heavy with the grape-like flowers of the wisteria vine and into the side door. Her thoughts drifted to that dreaded day they lost Claudio.

Something had pulled Rosa to the shoreline that afternoon. The clouds had rolled over Venice so quickly, leaving her with an eerie feeling. Once she made it to the bank, the rain blanketed the city.

Living on the island named after the famous Saint Erasmus, or Saint Elmo for short, she had a deep devotion to the patron saint of sailors. She would say a prayer every day when Claudio left for work. "Dear Saint Erasmus, protector of all seamen, please watch over Claudio today. May his paddle move swiftly and his gondola be protected against all danger. In Jesus' name, I pray. Amen."

She now said the same prayer for Leo. She wasn't upset he was going to the States for a little while. Every minute he was away from Venice was a minute she didn't have to worry about him on the water. Leo had taken Claudio's death the hardest out of her children. He couldn't find peace with the circumstances around it. She prayed she would see that care-free look in his eyes one day soon.

7

MAGGIE

Savannah, Georgia

Maggie let her hands drape over the sides of the kayak and into the water, enjoying the cool sensation running up her arms. The smell of saltwater, and the taste of it on her lips, made her remember why she loved this job. She felt complete when she was near the water; she was drawn to it like a magnet.

The sway of the kayak on the gentle waves threatened to lull her to sleep. She pulled up on the shore and decided to relax for the first time of the day. The stars were bright against the black sky. She propped her sleeping bag behind her, leaned back in the kayak, looked up into the heavens, and let her mind drift.

After years of being a cheerleader, she had a natural tendency to make people happy. When she graduated from Georgia Southern University, she traded her pom-poms for a business degree and had been very careful not to get too involved in other people's problems.

She had barely escaped the adventure group that evening. The group was made up of businessmen on a sales trip from Chicago. She knew they would be trouble when they had arrived early that morning complaining about the gnats and wearing their UPF 50 fishing shirts, still newly creased. Her business catered to many similar groups, and she was very thankful for the business, but she often felt like the mom to many ungrateful teenagers. On top of that, they weren't the most athletic group, either. Like most men in their mid-thirties, each was fighting a paunch, some more than others. They half-listened to the instructions while still on the beach, then pushed off towards Jack's Cut.

Halfway into the paddle, one of the men got knocked off his kayak. The wake of a fishing boat that he wasn't paying attention to completely overturned him. She had spent twenty minutes giving him a pep talk, trying to get him back on top of his kayak. "Come on, you're a big strong man. You've got this. Lean on the float that I put on the end of your paddle and use it as balance to pull yourself up." She eventually had to get into the water and give his backside the push it needed to get into the boat as the tide continued to take his fellow paddlers off course. Some people had no business on the many rivers around Savannah. *If you don't have the intelligence to show the water the respect and fear it deserves, then it might be better to stay ashore,* she had thought.

After herding the paddlers back together, Maggie decided to pull up on a closer island than she had previously planned. They had spent the rest of the day fishing and attempting to throw the cast net, but their fresh-catch dinner was sparse. She was thankful she had made a run to Russo's Seafood the night before.

The group drank the entire time Maggie cooked; as the last man fixed his plate, she popped open a beer. It was a hot August day; the cold beer washed the heat off immediately. The minute she sat down, eleven of the twelve men wanted to tell her their life story and give her some tidbit of advice about her own. It was that twelfth person who had intrigued her. The sadness in his eyes made him appear unapproachable, and she became determined to make him smile. She always wanted customers to leave happy. Truth be known, she was always trying to make others happy; it gave her joy. By the time he had unloaded both his money and marriage problems to Maggie, his whole demeanor had changed. She had succeeded once again. She always did.

She left the group to double-check their tents for the night and ensure they had the right amount of wood for the fire. Once she noticed the men were passing around bourbon, she left the group for the evening. She had seen it many times before; once bourbon comes out, all women better beware.

She paddled to a safe place around the cove. Thankfully, there was a good breeze blowing that evening. If not, the sand gnats would have eaten her up all night. She truly believed if she made it to purgatory, and she prayed to make it that far, gnats would be there to torture her for her atonement. After stargazing for a short while, she pulled her kayak further on the beach, grabbed her sleeping bag, and made her way to the hammock. She had found refuge in that hammock many times before; sometimes not alone.

She and Trevor had brought the 18' Scout to that spot

two years ago, right before their breakup. It had been an unusually high spring tide, and they hung the hammock high between two straggly palms to get out of the water. She briefly thought of his face and willed herself to stop before it was too late. When she was lonely, she would think of the morning he broke up with her and wonder if she should have gone after him. Thank goodness her dad had been there to stop her from making a fool of herself.

Maggie focused on her surroundings and got comfortable listening to the sound of the wind through the palms, which swayed her back and forth. She knew she would sleep peacefully; she always did when near the ocean.

MAGGIE WOKE before dawn and paddled around to the group. Mac had dropped off the cooler with supplies the night before; she cheated by pouring some lighter fluid on the wood to get the fire blazing. She placed an enormous blue speckled coffee pot over the open fire, praying the water would boil quickly to percolate. Next, she started to fry the thick-cut bacon. One by one, the men wandered from their tents and up to the fire, like moths to a flame. They looked like a much different group with red-rimmed eyes and day-old stubble than the men she had first met the previous morning. Bourbon will do that.

She fried eggs in the bacon grease, checked on the aluminum tray of pre-made biscuits she had placed on two bricks in the fire, and called everyone for breakfast. The group spread blankets on the beach and ate heartily. They would be picked up by the deep-sea fishing boat for the second leg of their trip in an hour, so she was in the home stretch. She radioed Mac to pick up the supplies and kayaks and started the clean-up process.

Mac was her right-hand man at the company, which had been won by a straight flush. Her dad had told her bits and pieces of the story. He had been in a serious late-night poker game and had laid down his shrimp boat as collateral. His opponent had laid down his kayak company. Her dad had won. Although she didn't know who the previous owner was, she knew they hadn't put much effort into their business. The property was several years behind in repairs and her dad only wished to be rid of it. Once he tied up his shrimp boat each day, the only work he wanted to do was lift his beer mug while sitting on his personalized stool at Dock's Bar. But Maggie saw the profitability in the long-term investment; she knew she could make it successful.

She had previously worked with a tour company in Savannah. Hired right out of college with her marketing degree in hand, she had planned to make Savannah the number one tourist destination in the States. It had become just that, but not by her efforts. Savannah was beautiful and mysterious. The weather was always comfortable, and the people were known for their hospitality. It also had the advantage of an open container policy, which tipped the scales when comparing cities for a golf trip or girl's weekend. For ten years, she had spent her days either behind a desk or driving a trolley. She was ready for a change and jumped at the opportunity to get paid for doing something she loved: kayaking.

Lazaretto River Sports, LRS for short, had been a shack with a run-down dock that sat on the deep water of

Lazaretto Creek. Its best assets were twenty kayaks that were practically brand new and an employee named Mac. He was an older gentleman, but capable of doing anything outdoors, so Maggie nicknamed him "Kangaroo Mac."

Having a marketing background, she knew how to advertise, and before she knew it, she was bringing in a profit. With all of Savannah's tourists, Maggie kept busy. The Girl Scouts who visited the home of its founder, Juliette Gordon Lowe, in downtown Savannah kept a steady flow of daily trips. Still, she decided to branch out to adventure tours, too. She gave Mac a nice raise and hired a few more guides, and things were going smoothly. If only the property wasn't haunted.

When Maggie first took over the business two years earlier, she held a grand opening celebration. Kathleen was the first person to leave the festivities. On her way out the door, she gently whispered to Maggie, "Girl, this place is majorly haunted and not just by one ghost. There are people speaking languages I can't put my finger on. You need to do some research on this place." She kissed her cheek and left quickly. Maggie understood Kathleen's quick departure; Kathleen was in touch with the spiritual world and always ran from it instead of embracing it. Some called her clairvoyant, but Kathleen brushed it off. Over the years, her friends just accepted that Kathleen could feel and see things they couldn't. But, unfortunately, Maggie felt and sometimes saw these ghosts, too. She knew that she should address it, but life came fast, and right now, she was busy trying to keep the company afloat.

8

THE PIRATE'S HOUSE

When she and Mac finally arrived at the office, she jumped in her jeep and ran home to shower and change. She was exhausted, but would never miss her Wednesday lunch with the tribe. Walking towards her front door, she was startled by a man sitting in one of her rockers on the porch. Front doors on Tybee were usually left open, so a waiting stranger scared her. His head was leaning back on one of her rocker cushions; he seemed to be taking a nap. She slowly turned toward her car when the stranger called out her name. "*Ciao, Maggie!*" with great exaggeration.

Maggie looked back a second time at the handsome man standing on her porch. Such dark hair and piercing green eyes; this was not a neighbor.

"Maggie, it's me, Leo," he said as he motioned to the house next door.

Leo? I don't know of any Leos, she thought. *And I'm not friends with anyone this handsome with an Italian accent...Wait a minute.* She looked him over once more. "Oh my gosh! *Leo* from next door!" They walked quickly towards one another, each surveying the other and smiling as they appreciated what they saw. "You're sure not that skinny boy I spent the summer with years ago. How long ago was that?"

"It was a lifetime ago; that's all I know. Sorry I startled you." He smiled and opened his arms for a hug. Maggie happily walked into his embrace and was surprised by the flutter in her heart. He let his hands slide down her arms until they connected with her hands. Smiling, he said, "You sure don't look like that tomboy who could spit watermelon seeds farther than me. Can I take you to lunch?"

The blush crept up her neck and quickly covered her entire face. She hated how she would blush from a compliment and hoped he hadn't noticed. "I'm actually dashing in my house to change and meet some friends for lunch. Girl-friends," she added, struck once again by how handsome he was. "How about dinner?"

He nodded and looked her over one last time, lingering on the small angel-wing tattoo on the inside of her ankle and smiled with approval. "Dinner sounds great."

"Walk over after five, and we can go from here. I'm so happy to see you." She hugged him once more before walking towards the door. She felt his eyes watching her. She looked back as she closed the door, and he waved before walking away.

While getting ready for lunch, she began to hum in the shower, something that she hadn't done in a very long time.

MAGGIE WAVED to Jan as she got out of her car. They linked arms as they walked up to The Pirates House together. It was one of the best-known restaurants in Savannah and every tourist's favorite. Still, the tribe was quickly growing tired of it. Agnes, however, absolutely loved the place, so they weren't surprised when she had chosen to eat there for the third time this year.

Their group of six met every Wednesday at 11:30 for lunch. They had become friends on their first day at Saint Vincent's, the all-girls Catholic high school in downtown Savannah. During their four years there, the group traveled as a pack and referred to themselves as the "tribe" of friends. Upon graduation, they all went their separate ways, off to find their place in the world. Like the sea turtles on Tybee, they each made their way back to where they were born — Savannah. Once home, they decided to meet once a week for lunch. They each took turns choosing the restaurant and footing the bill.

When they entered the front door, Stephanie and Kathleen were sitting on an extended bench, waiting to be seated. Latrice was standing beside the life-size wooden pirate. She winked at them and looked up at the pirate, "So where've you been all my life, or at least for the last six weeks since we've been here?" They all laughed, each adding to the fun. "It's amazing what they've done with the place," "Déjà vu!", "The third time's a charm."

The friendly hostess, dressed in a barmaid costume, came and escorted the five of them to the table where Agnes was waiting, complete with an eye patch and pirate hat. She had memorized The Pirate's House welcome, given to her frequently as a child, and stood to welcome the five of them. "Welcome to The Pirate's House, ARRGG!"

"No way!" Kathleen muttered to the group.

"Way!" they all answered in unison. This banter was something they always did to keep everybody included in a conversation.

Agnes walked to the front of their table. "In the mid-1700s, this very building was an inn and tavern for many sailors and privateers; some of them may or may not have been pirates. There are tunnels dug right under our feet. Pirates once smuggled rum, and whatever sailors they could wrangle, down these tunnels and onto their pirate ships. One of Savannah's local policemen, who came in for a quick drink one night, fell victim to these pirates. It took him over two years to make his way back from China."

She took a deep breath, looked each of them in the eyes, and continued. "Famous author, Robert Louis Stevenson, is said to have written some of his novel, *Treasure Island,* when he visited The Pirates' House. He wrote about Captain John Flint, who had buried his loot on an island and hid it with a treasure map. The captain died in Savannah from drinking too much rum, and his map was given to Billy Bones, who began the great search." Agnes took one more break then spoke very quietly. "Many-a-ghost from the past roam these rooms at night. Spirits of pirates and the people that met their sword. Don't be caught wandering upstairs and never, ever, go into the tunnels below alone."

The people around them started clapping at the tables, and the tribe joined in. Several of the children in the room sat up a little taller, either looking for adventure or for ghosts, and the bar maiden hostess actually said, "Wow, I didn't know all that stuff." Then she walked off, shoulders back, proud to be wearing the barmaid outfit.

Agnes nodded with a satisfied grin and sat down. "I know y'all think I'm crazy, always choosing The Pirates' House, but this place just makes me happy. The only time I remember going to a restaurant was coming here because it entertained my three older brothers. I wanted you to experience it like I once did, with some background information about why it's just so cool. Since they no longer do the welcome speech, I decided to give it to you."

Stephanie jumped in, "God bless your mama raising your crazy brothers. Gosh, they tortured us in high school."

"They sure did," Jan added, shaking her head, "but thank goodness they stayed on you, Agnes, or you wouldn't have landed that basketball scholarship to Notre Dame."

Agnes nodded briefly, "You're right. Remind me to thank them for the years of slamming my shots in the driveway." She let out a small sigh, then held out the pirate gear. "Now put on your pirate hats, and let's eat."

While everyone ordered cocktails, Kathleen asked, "So, who's coming to the Rockin' in the School Year party at Forsyth on Saturday? Jack told me to ask you guys over a couple of hours before for cocktails, and then we can walk to the park at eight."

"I'm in," said Agnes. "Back-to-school parties are the best, especially for parents. Hey, do y'all remember last year when the Chippewas' lead singer fell off the stage?"

"Yeah, and when he got back on stage, he kept climbing to the very top of all the speakers with blood running down his face from his fall," exclaimed Latrice.

Agnes continued, "Well, I heard they were the headliners this year. I can't wait to see them."

Everyone around the table agreed and said they were going, except for Jan, who had become unusually quiet. "I'll meet up with you guys there. I have something to do before," she said, and then quickly changed the subject. "What else is new?"

Maggie jumped in telling them about her exciting visitor and they all sat up to listen. "The summer before high school, the sweet Italian couple who lived next to my grandmother's house on Tybee had family come to visit them from Italy. They were amazing, and I loved having kids my age to play with. The oldest boy, Leo, and I really hit it off, and we ran the streets all summer long. When I got home this morning from a kayak overnight, Leo was sitting in a rocking chair on my front porch. Long story short, we are going to dinner tonight."

Everyone immediately started teasing her, but she shook them off. "It's not like that. Really, it's not." But her mind went to that summer and the awkward goodbye kiss between two fourteen-year-olds; she smiled, wondering if Leo remembered that kiss, too.

9

OKRA'S VENGEANCE

Maggie was ready for dinner early, so she passed the time in her garden. She hadn't walked the yard since before the kayak trip and needed to pick the ripe tomatoes before the birds got them. She grabbed her floppy hat, garden basket, and pruning shears, slid on her clogs, and walked towards the garden. Her steps quickened at the sight of the deep red tomatoes and bright yellow squash from across the yard. She always planted the vegetables during Holy Week. Her grandmother had taught her to have the plants in the ground before Good Friday to get the best harvest. That one trick had continued to work in her favor, and even in early August, her garden was still producing a full weekly basket.

One minute in the garden turned to thirty minutes, and before she knew it, she had a basket full of vegetables and dirt under her nails. She was carefully following the path past the okra when she saw Leo walking in the back gate. As she raised her free hand to wave, her gardening clog got caught on the neighboring cucumber vine, and she stumbled into the patch of okra. Her basket of vegetables tumbled out everywhere. But worse than that, the okra plants that broke her fall had rubbed against both of her forearms. She inwardly groaned, knowing the okra fibers caused a terrible reaction to her skin.

Leo ran to the garden to help her up and teased, "Are you falling for me already?" She smiled into his bright green eyes. Although she immediately began to itch, she decided she wouldn't scratch or complain.

Leo immediately started admiring his surroundings, commenting on each plant as he carefully put the spilled produce back into the basket. "You have a beautiful garden," he said as he plucked a bright orange zucchini flower, brushed it clean, and popped it into his mouth.

Maggie's stomach flip-flopped as she watched him eat from her garden. It felt so intimate that something she planted and cared for was being enjoyed with such fervor. She watched his lips curl into a smile as he hummed with appreciation, and for a brief second, she wished she was that flower. *Simmer down, girl*, she told herself and tore her gaze from him.

No one except Kathleen ever enjoyed her garden, so Leo's appreciation filled her with pride. She smiled, thinking back to when the tribe had come to Tybee for the 4th of July. Stephanie had followed her to the garden with a glass of wine while Maggie cut fresh basil for a Caprese salad. Stephanie had looked at one of the tomato plants, whose tomatoes had not yet ripened, and said, "Hey, this is cool. You planted green tomatoes this year. I sure do love me some fried green tomatoes." Maggie had laughed, thinking she was joking, but she just nodded in agreement after noticing Stephanie's face was serious. It always amazed her that Stephanie was such a brilliant engineer and could fix anything in the world, but her knowledge of everyday things was sparse.

This was definitely not one of those moments. Leo not only knew the vegetables, but he also knew zucchini flowers were tasty treats.

When the produce had been returned to the basket, she asked, "How do you know so much about vegetables? I thought you were going to be a gondolier?"

"My mom's side of the family comes from generations of gardeners. We live on Sant' Erasmus Island, off the coast of Venice. While my father trained me to be a gondolier, the rest of my family farms the land for produce which is distributed all over the Veneto region." He slowly looked around the backyard as he spoke, so Maggie began to show him around.

Most of her yard was shaded and held many hostas, ferns, and gingers tucked away in various areas. Her grandmother had Lady Bank roses covering the fences; Maggie had added black-eyed susan vines, which had taken over one whole side of the house. Although they were beautiful, the vines ran everywhere, trying to find somewhere to attach their tendrils.

Her yard backed up to the bend of a creek with two large oak trees hanging over the water. It held a small fifteen-foot walkway that led to a floating dock where she kept some of the kayaks. On one side of the walkway were two Adirondack chairs that were completely shaded and just waiting for someone to come and relax in them. On the other side was a birdbath used as a planter for the many colors of portulaca. In its center stood a concrete statue of the Holy Family.

Leo motioned to the statuary, "The Holy Family. Nice."

"It's been here for as long as I can remember. My grandmother would always tell me how the devil was scared of a holy marriage." She finished the rest of her grandmother's statement silently in her head. *And that I should always look for a holy man like Saint Joseph to marry.*

Leo let his eyes wander around the yard, appreciating what it must feel like to be part of Maggie's world, then they continued to wander around. Maggie stopped at the back porch, sat the vegetables on a small table, and grabbed two Tybee Island Blonde beers from the outdoor refrigerator. She took off her hat and rubbed the cool of the bottle against the back of her neck before opening it. The first sip was always the best; she savored the moment then sighed. As they finished walking the perimeter of the house, Leo acknowledged that her taste in plants was more wild and whirly than her grandmother's had been. Still, the combination made for a perfect yard.

They began to walk the five blocks towards AJ's for dinner. It was always packed in the summer, but they could grab an outdoor table that sat right over the water. After another beer, the Low Country Boil was brought to their table. They began peeling the shrimp, one after another.

Maggie winced in pain as the salty drippings from the Old Bay on the shrimp made the sting on her arms intensify. When she looked down, she was horrified to see huge welts. Leo noticed them at the same time and gently took her hands into his for a better examination. Concern spread across his face. "Any idea where this rash came from?"

Embarrassed, she explained how her body reacts to okra and how she had been hiding it from him all night so it wouldn't ruin their evening. She was upset with herself for not handling it when it happened and was on the verge of tears.

Leo moved his barstool around to her side of the table. He spun her towards him, so they were sitting face to face. Calmly taking two towels off the table, he poured his ice water onto both, then poured the vinegar on the table for the fish & chips onto the towels, too. He placed them around both of her arms and held them in place. Their knees touched while she bounced her legs nervously. He decided to try to distract her while the vinegar did its magic by telling her a story.

"I remember the first time I met you. My parents were playing cards, and I was being a nuisance. They ran me out of the house, telling me to walk over and meet the little girl next door. I didn't want to play with dolls or Barbies, so I was in no hurry to meet you. But, I did as I was told. Instead of walking to the front, I jumped the fence in the backyard and found you standing on the dock, throwing a cast net. You held one of its edges between your teeth and grasped the other ends so expertly that when you spun around, it fanned out perfectly. It looked like magic. I stood and watched in awe as you pulled it up and emptied your catch into a bucket. Right then and there, I knew that American girls were much different from Italian girls, and I couldn't wait to know you better. What I didn't understand was that it wasn't all American girls who were different; it was just you."

Her knees stopped bouncing as she relaxed, listening intently. Before she knew it, she hadn't thought about her arms for over ten minutes. She was lost entirely in Leo's words. He slowly lifted the towels when he finished talking, and the rash was gone.

"How did you do that?" she asked.

"The fibers in the okra irritated your skin, and the salty drippings from the shrimp made it worse. Vinegar counteracts the sting of the fibers, and the water cooled you down. Do you feel better?"

She smiled, "Yes, I'm completely better." *Better than I've been for a very long time*, she thought to herself. Then, remembering what he had said when he entered her garden earlier, she added. "Maybe falling for you wasn't so bad, huh?" They both laughed as he slowly moved his chair back to his side of the table and then devoured what was left of the shrimp.

10

ROCKIN' IN THE SCHOOL YEAR

Maggie pushed open the back gate at Kathleen's downtown home on Jones Street and felt the familiar tingle of the excitement of entering her outside garden. Much different from the expanse of Maggie's yard, Kathleen had perfectly fit her love of nature into a small space that had been laid out to feel airy and open. It was beautiful with a pool, statues, water features, and a small kitchen garden. It was shaded by large oaks, so it felt incredible even on a hot August day.

The smell of Confederate Jasmine that grew along the brick wall filled the air and mingled with the sound of Jazz music playing. Her children were dressed in their pajamas. They had been splashing around the pool during the day, and their hair was still damp. Maggie had a chance to tickle and chase them a bit before Kathleen took them upstairs for their grandmother to put them to sleep. Kathleen had asked everyone to bring an hors d'oeuvre, and Kathleen's husband, Jack, made his famous Bahama Mamas.

"So, what's up with Jan? She seemed so secretive about meeting up with us tonight," asked Stephanie.

"She always acts that way when there's a new man in her life. I bet that's what it is," Kathleen added.

"No way!" Maggie said.

"Way!" the group said in unison and laughed. Kathleen added, "We will find out soon enough."

As it approached 8 p.m, the tribe began to walk down the brick sidewalk along Jones Street towards Forsyth Park. They began hearing the band's drums and the crowd's cheers as they passed Taylor Street, indicating there was a good turnout this year.

The group walked down the side of the park and mingled their way to an open spot in the middle of the crowd, spread out blankets in the grass, and got comfortable. The park was full of people; families, high school and college kids, old-timers, and every age in between. Everyone had turned out to listen to the four bands, each playing their different styles of music for fifteen minutes, leading up to the headliner, The Chippewas.

The MC kept the flow of the evening moving smoothly. The fourth band played jazz, and they wrapped up their set with "What a Wonderful World." Louis Armstrong himself would have been proud of their performance, and the crowd rewarded them with a standing ovation. As the tribe got to their feet, Agnes began nudging the others while pointing to the side of the stage. There stood Jan with an arm draped around her shoulder. They all stared in disbelief as bad-boy Eddie Simon, the leader of the Chippewas, whispered in sweet Jan's ear.

"I wasn't sure it was Jan at first, but I recognized her

outfit," Agnes explained. Jan was an artist inside and out, and she dressed accordingly. She loved the most colorful clothing and often wore matching hats and shoes. Although no one else could pull off one of her outfits, the ensembles looked adorable on Jan.

After seeing Jan with Eddie, the group quickly understood why Jan was being so secretive and meeting them at the park.

As the Chippewas began to set up, the group took the opportunity to refill their drinks. Maggie was elbow-deep with her tush in the air, digging in the cooler, searching for her favorite drink. She didn't notice the hush of the group until she popped up, holding a Mike's Hard Lemonade in the air with excitement. She leaned back to see Leo standing at the edge of the cooler, looking down at her. He nodded, then addressed her friends, "*Buona sera*, ladies. Maggie said I could join you all tonight."

The tribe all welcomed Leo to the group, and Jack stood to shake his hand. Then Jack asked Maggie to pull a Peroni from the cooler for Leo. Jack had become hooked on the beer when they were in Italy the year prior, so he had Ganem's Liquor Store on Habersham keep them in stock for him. Leo was embarrassed that Maggie was getting him a drink, so he bent over the same time she did. They collided, causing Maggie to lose her balance and fall backward on the ground. Leo quickly scooped her up in his arms, holding her for a bit longer than they both expected, and placed her in a standing position. He then helped brush her off.

Maggie felt everyone's eyes upon them. She turned to notice the gaping mouths of all of her friends as they stared in a rare moment of silence. The sting of a blush slowly spread across her face as she pushed her hair back behind her ears and thanked Leo.

"Some say gallantry is dead, but you just proved them wrong. Good show, Leo!" Agnes blurted out, and the rest of the group chimed in with approval. Over the past two years, Maggie had introduced her friends to different people she was interested in. Still, they never fit in with the group. Trevor had a close relationship with her friends, and she began to worry that she would never find anyone like that again. But as she looked at the smiles on their faces, she felt a tinge of hope. She decided to throw down her guard and just be herself, so she opened her hard lemonade and drank it a little too quickly. The sweet lemon flavor went down easy on a hot evening. Leo was very comfortable in his own skin. He stretched out in the grass, slowly sipping on the Peroni, and seemed to feel right at home.

Eddie still had the touch. He was an excellent singer and guitarist. His band played everything: 80's, rock 'n' roll, and more modern music. The last song of the evening was performed by a combination of all five bands. Eddie pulled Jan on the stage with him as the group played "Georgia on My Mind."

The tribe rushed the stage and stood in front of Jan. They were all swaying and singing. As the song ended, Jan looked to them, held up her "Rock On" sign, winked, and blew them a kiss. Eddie Simon watched her, then followed her eyes over to them, and he did the same. He blew them a kiss and held up the "Rock On" sign. They all screamed like groupies and couldn't stop laughing.

11

THE BELLS OF MASS

M aggie was dreaming she was swimming in the middle of the ocean. Looking ahead, she could see the tall red sea buoy, which was swaying back and forth and ringing like a bell. She swam as hard as she could, trying to get closer. "Gong. gong. gong," it rang, but as hard as she swam, she couldn't close the distance. "Gong, gong," it sang again. The gonging slowly changed into the ring of her phone as she fought her way into consciousness. She worked hard to lift her eyelids, which seemed to weigh 100 pounds. "Who lets the phone ring that many times without hanging up?" she muttered.

Her head pounded from too many libations at the concert, and her mind was still treading water from her dream. She knew who was calling because she called every Sunday morning. "Good morning, Kathleen. I'm walking out the door to church right now." Then she hung up quickly before Kathleen asked her any questions.

Every Saturday, Maggie begged Kathleen to call and

make sure she was awake for Mass on Sunday, and every Sunday morning, she wished she hadn't. Today was definitely no exception. She got out of bed, still sore from swimming to the buoy in her sleep. Or, more than likely, from dancing in the park. She jumped into the shower, towel-dried her hair, and threw on one of her many sundresses with sandals. The church was only four blocks away, so she made the short walk quickly. Every Sunday morning, the small Tybee church offered two Masses, 9:00 and 10:30. Every Marian feast day, they prayed the Rosary between Masses at the grotto out front. Although they had advertised it after Mass last weekend, she had forgotten that it was the Feast of the Assumption. She was surprised when she walked up to the many parishioners gathered out front. She cursed under her breath and immediately regretted it.

As she got closer, she recognized Leo standing in the back with an older lady on each side. She began to fidget, suddenly questioning her dress choice. His dark hair blew in the beach breeze, and she watched as he tried to push it in place. He looked up and made eye contact just as the congregation began the third decade. He motioned for her to come and stand by him and reached out his hand as she got closer, smiling as she joined in. As the Hail Holy Queen ended the Rosary, she looked down to notice them still holding hands. She had never openly prayed with a man before, and she was shocked at how the intimacy of it stirred her soul.

As people began to disperse, he said, "I was persuaded to go to early Mass this morning. The young ladies over there are taking me to Sunrise Cafe." As the Mass bell began to ring, Maggie said, "I'd better get moving before they lock the doors on me. Enjoy your breakfast." She made her way into the church, but caught a quick look back at the group slowly walking down Butler Avenue to breakfast. Leo was in the center, helping the others along the sidewalk whether they needed help or not. His jet-black hair in the middle of their sea of white hair, made Maggie smile. They were each beaming and doting on him like he was the best thing since sliced bread.

On her walk home from Mass, Maggie planned the rest of her Sunday. Most Tybee businesses made their money on the weekends between March and September when the throngs of visitors took over the beach. However, she always closed Lazaretto River Sports on Sundays. She could still hear her grandmother say, "Keep holy the Sabbath," and it made her happy when she did. She also noticed a difference when people returned to work on Monday. They were rested and grateful for the time off.

Maggie's parents weren't around a lot when she was younger. Her mom worked at the hospital, often taking double shifts and picking up extra time. She told Maggie that raising a family was expensive. Still, as Maggie got older, she decided her mom just loved being a nurse. She was good at it, too. Her mom always encouraged Maggie to do well in school, saying her education could never be taken away. She was right, of course, but Maggie's mom didn't realize that also applied in other areas. Memories and time spent with your children could never be taken away either, but those were things that her mom hadn't made a priority.

Her dad picked up the pieces and played the role of both mom and dad most of the time, but his weaknesses was found inside a bottle. The shrimp boat was the only thing that didn't put conditions on him and became his place of refuge. He invited Maggie into his world often. Some of her fondest memories were made sitting on the bench seat of his boat, watching the seagulls following closely behind as he opened the boat's outriggers. Her dad saw Maggie as she truly was, not just a girl who was clever or pretty. In fact, sometimes she felt like he didn't even see her as a girl at all; he only saw her as a child of the Low Country.

Her dad noticed the look in her eyes when she was on the water and her natural ability to swim, get muddy, and fish. He called her his "river rat," a name that would irk her mom to no end, but it thrilled Maggie. She spent most of her summers with him on the boat and acted as his co-captain. She stayed out of the way of his deck hands, whose jobs were to get the doors and nets in the water and to watch closely as the wench pulled in the catch. It was Maggie's job to examine the catch. Although the nets had the devices in place for fish and sea turtles to escape, they always seemed to catch odds and ends that needed to be put back into the water. The faster Maggie could return the sea life to the water, the better their chance of survival.

After a day on the water, her dad would take her to her grandmother's house, where she would stay almost every night. Sometimes, depending on the size of the day's catch, he might not make it back until the following day to pick up Maggie. As she got older, she realized that her dad always celebrated a large haul with a large alcohol intake, and sometimes it lasted for days. She learned to take the good with the bad, and the good always included her grandmother.

Her grandmother was her constant. Maggie still missed her every day. She was beyond grateful for all the things she learned from her, and the lesson for the day was to keep holy the Sabbath. Wanting to talk to family, she called her parents, but got their answering machine. Although not surprised, she felt lonely. She took a book onto the back porch, but kept being interrupted by the sounds coming from next door. First the roar of the lawnmower, then the knock of a hammer. She smiled at the thought of Leo taking care of his family and hoped his sweet aunt was inside relaxing on her Sunday.

12

HORSE PEN CREEK

Maggie sat at her desk, looking over the schedule for the upcoming week. Lazaretto River Sports was finally breaking even, but she still held her breath every Monday when she went over the books. She felt his presence before she saw him; when she looked up from the computer, Leo was standing in front of her, smiling. He held up a small bag and a cup of coffee. "Good morning. I brought you something." She opened the bag, letting the aroma fill the air, and started tapping her feet as she reached inside. Then, she let out a long sigh when she took a bite.

"Your aunt's cheese danish, Mmm, delicious. She doesn't make them often, so you must be working really hard for her." She took another bite and enjoyed the flaky, buttery pastry with the sweet ricotta and mascarpone with lemon zest. "Well, my Monday morning just took a turn for the better."

"I hope that's because of me, not the pastry," Leo said with a sheepish grin.

She smiled and motioned Leo to a chair across from hers. "You've got my full attention. What's up?"

He fidgeted in his chair, then looked her in the eye, asking, "Would you be hiring?"

She had not expected him to ask for a job and was both surprised and intrigued. Why would a gondolier from Venice want to work as a kayak instructor? She pushed her questions aside and nodded, "Yes, we are. Most of my instructors are leaving since summer is coming to an end, either to go back to college or find more money in our slower season. So, we have spots available. I know you appreciate the water, but have you ever kayaked?"

"No. But I'm a quick learner."

Maggie considered his offer. "Why don't you walk over to my house this afternoon, and we'll go for a quick paddle to give you the basics. Then I'll get you to shadow Mac for the next couple of weeks to learn about group control and safety."

A smile spread across his face, "That would be wonderful. Thank you so much, Maggie. I'll see you this afternoon." They shook hands, and she watched him walk away. Maggie tried getting back to the work piled on her desk, but her thoughts kept drifting to Leo. "What's his story?" she mumbled, remembering a conversation she had with his uncle next door before he passed away. He told her how proud he was of his brother, the gondolier. He was some sort of prestigious gondolier for an important family in Venice. It was an honor and would be passed to his son, so why would Leo want to be a kayak instructor on Tybee? She knew it was none of her business, but she was very curious. Then she started questioning herself. *Why am I so inter-*

ested? She realized she was grinning. Was she falling for Leo?

THAT AFTERNOON, as they walked to the dock, a tabby cat dashed across the yard chasing a squirrel from Maggie's garden. After climbing an overhanging palm tree, the squirrel gained courage and looked down at the cat while screeching at him in squirrel language.

"Looks like the cat is your own personal scarecrow," Leo said, laughing at the squirrel still screaming at the feline.

Maggie snickered, "That's Joe. He brings me all the bandits from my yard. I've had birds, crickets, lizards, fiddler crabs, and snakes all delivered to my back porch door."

"A cat named Joe?" Leo asked.

"I found him on the Feast of St. Joseph." Maggie shrugged her shoulders and felt Leo's stare. "So Joe it was," she finished. When she met Leo's eyes, he quickly turned his attention back to the cat who had chased a grasshopper deep into the lemongrass.

As they walked to the bluff, Maggie explained how she dragged the kayaks to the dock and slid them into the water. But Leo lifted his and slowly placed it in the creek. He explained, "My father's family has a tiny piece of property on Canal Rio Della Sensa in Venice. It's been passed down in the family and was given to me by my father when I became a gondolier. The place itself is ancient and needs repairs, but the property has a dock where I keep the boat that I run back and forth from Sant' Erasmus, where I live. This reminds me of that place."

"Do you love Venice?" Maggie asked.

Sadness came across his eyes before he answered, "I once did." Then he quickly changed the subject. He looked around the dock and spotted the paddles. "I believe you must instruct me a little."

She explained the kayaks they used were cockpit kayaks. Unlike the sit-on-tops they used for the day excursions, these were more comfortable as the water got colder and could be used all year. "It takes a lot to flip them unless you try to stand in them. So, Mr. Gondolier, you need to stay seated. Can you do that?"

"I think I can handle it," he said with a grin.

That morning after Leo left her office, she had done a little research on the paddles that gondoliers used, so she then explained the paddle to Leo. "Unlike the remo, you are familiar with, this oar has a paddle at each end, and there is no fórcola to lock it into. You hold it in both hands and pull hard on each side. It becomes second nature once you're on the water, so we should just start. It should come really easy to you. Just watch for boats coming in and out of the creek."

He smiled, "Remo? Fórcola? You've been doing some research on me?" he teased.

"Just get in and show me what you got," she answered as they shoved off, riding the current out of Horse Pen Creek in the direction she wanted to go. They paddled side by side, going slow while Leo got accustomed to the paddle in his hand. While they paddled, Maggie introduced the topic that he seemed to be having a hard time discussing. "I was so sorry to hear about your dad. Your aunt was upset she couldn't make the funeral."

"My dad was a great man. I don't think I realized how

much I depended on him until he was no longer there," he replied but kept paddling. Then he added, "Everybody keeps telling me it's going to get easier, and I keep waiting for that time, but I had to get out of Venice. It's just too hard."

Maggie nodded her head, "I'm so sorry, Leo. I was only around your dad a few times, but he really was amazing."

Leo thought about his kind dad and how he lived by the motto, "Always do the right thing." He worried his dad would be very disappointed in him for running from Venice. His mind drifted straight to the accident, and he felt the shame. Would he ever be able to think about his dad without mingling the accident in his memory?

Maggie watched Leo, who was completely lost in his thoughts. She could solve so many problems while on the water. The rhythm of the paddle hitting the water was one of the most peaceful things on earth. She prayed Leo would find some peace kayaking today. His eyes were solemnly set, causing a crease on the bridge of his nose. She felt sorrow for his grieving heart.

They had begun slow, traveling side by side while he got accustomed to the paddle in hand, but after a few minutes, he was moving strong. Many first timers move zigzag, reacting to the pull of the paddle, but he pulled steadily through the water with even strength on both sides and went perfectly straight. He paddled vigorously as if trying to get away from his past, and Maggie struggled to keep up. As the creek dumped out into the much larger river, they rested the paddles in their laps and glided.

His serious face changed into a smile. "That was awesome!" She nodded her head in agreement, and he continued by asking, "Now, where does this river go?"

"This river goes straight out to the Atlantic Ocean," she answered.

"This river goes to the sea?" he asked. She shook her head no and was briefly considering explaining the differences between seas and oceans when he splashed her with his paddle. Naturally, she had to return the favor.

As they pulled their kayaks onto the sandy shore of the Back River, she was thankful for the quiet of a Monday afternoon. They practically had the beach to themselves. They dove into the water to cool off and then relaxed on the sand along the shoreline.

"What about you, Maggie? What's your story?" he asked.

She gave a deep sigh, "Well, I've been in a very long-term relationship that I thought would end in marriage until, well, it didn't. I haven't dated much in the last year because I spend most of my time at LRS, but I really want the whole husband and family thing. I'm almost scared that I missed my chance." *Where did that come from?* she wondered. She hadn't said that out loud to anyone. How could she speak so freely to a man she barely knew?

"You haven't missed your chance; you still have plenty of time. Maybe, you just haven't found the right person." Their eyes met; she was embarrassed by his comment, but smiled.

His face turned serious once again, and he blurted out, "There was an accident." His abruptness captured her full attention. He explained the whole scene as it had been explained to him many times by the police, but it always ended the same, with his father's death. "I have so many questions, and things just don't add up. Every day it gets worse and worse to be on the canal with people who are so unkind; I can hardly make myself get out of bed in the mornings to go to a job that I once loved. One day, when I was at my lowest, I saw a dolphin. We've never had dolphins in Venice before, so it was a big surprise. I thought about Savannah, and here I am."

"Yes, you are," Maggie said. "The newest tour guide for Lazaretto River Sports. People are going to line up to have a gondolier as their instructor."

"I don't know about that, but I do know how much I love the water." He stood and dove out into deeper water and began to float on his back. She had never met anyone as drawn to the water as she was, and his fascination intrigued her. Maggie wasn't sure how long he would be in Savannah, but she would enjoy his company while he was there.

13

THE NEW GUIDE

Maggie tapped the steering wheel to the beat of a song playing on her favorite 80's station. Each tune held so many memories. She listened to the station every Wednesday on her way to meet the tribe and thought about fun memories she had shared with her group of friends.

She drove to River Street because Latrice had chosen the Olympia Cafe for lunch. It was a favorite for the group of six because it was owned by a friendly family who always took care of their regulars. The husband, Mr. Diakos, had immigrated from Greece and had once played for their Olympic soccer team. He was full of personality and would have a bottle of ouzo sitting in the middle of the table waiting for them. Today was no exception.

The ladies started off with dolmadakia, stuffed grape leaves, Mr. Diakos' recommendation for the day. They all picked off the Greek antipasto plate, enjoying the chilled

Greek olives and artichoke hearts that were perfect for the 100-degree heat. For the main course, they devoured souvlaki pork skewers and sauteed shrimp and scallops over couscous.

As they waited for dessert, they heard the long deep whistle from a passing ship, so Mr. Diakos shooed them outside to watch her pass. They walked onto the cobble-stones of River Street just in time to see the massive ship moving along in front of the restaurant heading out of port. Although they all lived in Savannah, they never tired of seeing that wondrous sight. As it passed, they listened to the smaller tugboats toot their horns, and they giggled at the difference. Latrice bragged about her lunch destination saying, "That's why you can never go wrong eating on River Street. Our city is so pretty."

"You can never go wrong eating on River Street because your office is in City Hall," Kathleen teased and nudged Latrice with her elbow. Latrice rolled her eyes in response.

"I wonder if Trevor knew you were at the Olympia Cafe, so he decided to do a drive-by?" Agnes asked. Maggie shook her head and rolled her eyes. There were no drive-bys on the enormous container ships that came into the Savannah port. The vessel seemed to be the same width of the channel, or so it appeared, and required perfect timing to pass other ships in certain areas.

"I hate that I liked him. He was like one of us. Jerk!" Stephanie exclaimed.

"I wonder how he's doing?" Jan asked.

The group all turned to Kathleen, waiting for an answer, while Maggie feigned disinterest.

Kathleen held up her hands. "All right. All right. Jack had lunch with him last week. You know they've been friends forever. I can't just demand Jack to stop liking him, although he was pretty pissed after he..., well, after the break-up. Anyway, Jack said he's doing fine. He finished his apprentice-ship and has been piloting on his own now for almost a year. His life has really slowed down. He's not seeing anyone and Jack said he really misses you. He said he wouldn't stop talking about you."

All eyes moved to Maggie. She quietly bit her lip for a brief second, then shook her head, thinking about the river pilot who still held a piece of her heart, and wondered when the hurt would completely go away. She automatically looked up to the bridge of the ship, like he had taught her to do, and was surprised when she saw his white-blonde hair. He was holding his binoculars in hand and waving straight at her. She lifted her hand in a slight wave and said, "It's best to leave the past in the past, now let's go get dessert and another ouzo for me."

As soon as they sat back down, Mr. Diakos brought out their favorite dessert of baklava and served it with Ellinikos kafes. As they each left, Mr. Diakos waved and said, "Ya!" to them, saying both 'goodbye' and 'see you soon' in that one little phrase. Once again, the Olympia Cafe didn't disappoint.

Maggie was sad on her ride back to Tybee, just like she always was after she saw Trevor. Six years was a very long time to spend with someone for them to walk out with no explanation. She had been stuck for so long, mainly because she never got closure. He never cared enough to even tell her why. She started to replay that morning, but then the strangest thing happened, she thought of Leo. It shocked her so much that she actually smiled. That was definitely a first because usually, the sad times lasted for days. Then she repeated what she had said earlier with the girls, but this time she meant it. "It's best to leave the past in the past."

LEO HAD BEEN SHADOWING Mac on each trip, and the two men had become fast friends. When they weren't on the water together, they banged around in the workshop behind the building. Mac had told her that morning, before leaving work, that Leo was ready for his own group, but she wanted to see for herself. She asked Leo to meet her back at LRS at 5 p.m.; she was more excited than she probably should have been.

Leo put their kayaks in at Lazaretto Creek, just as he would if he led a group. As they made their way out towards the mouth of the creek, Maggie let him take the lead, and he watched her in his peripheral vision, keeping an eye on where she was in the river. Leo was a natural, and she knew he would be a great guide.

"So, why is this creek named Lazaretto?" he asked.

"I'm not really sure. Why?"

"'Lazaretto' means...," he stumbled with his English. "It means an institution for people with a disease, like a hospital. Is there a hospital at the other end of this creek?"

Maggie laughed, "No, there isn't a hospital on Tybee. We go all the way to town if there is an emergency. I'm sure it's just a coincidence."

Leo nodded, but Maggie could tell that he was still thinking about the creek's name. On the way back in, they passed the Cockspur Lighthouse, and Leo wanted to explore. The tide was low enough to bank their kayaks near the rocks, so she agreed. Many of the groups would paddle beside the lighthouse and as a guide, he should know its history.

"The lighthouse was built in the 1850s. It was built at the entrance of this shallow south channel and used to guide the vessels into the port," she explained.

"But the ships do not come this way. I've watched them from the top of Fort Pulaski," he said.

"You're right," she said with a grin. "Over time, as the ships became more sizable and needed a deeper route, the vessels began using the North channel. The lighthouse hasn't been operational since 1909. Let's go see it."

The smell of dead fish and birds was overwhelming as they walked inside, and they both cringed at the stench. The stairs no longer made it to the top, but there was a small window halfway up that people could still look out. While they were inside, she kept thinking she heard people talking, but she only saw their kayaks when she looked out the window. Then she heard it, the five short blows of the ship's horn. She looked at the kayaks again, noticed the water running out, and started running towards the door.

"Leo, get to the boats," she yelled, and he followed behind her.

She then heard Trevor's voice, the one she knew so well, roaring over the two-way radio, "Maggie, what the hell are you doing? Get out of there." After a split second, he must have seen Leo running behind her because he simply added, "Ohhhh!"

Trevor was not her present problem; she and Leo had to act quickly. They jumped in the kayaks and paddled towards the middle of the creek as fast as they could. When they finally stopped, they looked back to watch the water crash against the lighthouse.

"We would have been smashed," Leo said in surprise.

"It would have knocked us, for sure, and would have definitely taken our kayaks," she answered.

Leo shook his head and asked, "How did you know?"

She explained, "The ships are so large. When they are in a channel, they push tons of water behind them, creating a depression in the front. The water fills the depression by pulling away from the shoreline, kinda like a tsunami. But, just like a tsunami, when it fills back in, it comes in with a vengeance." Maggie was irritated with herself. "I know better. I should have been more careful. That's how accidents happen on the water when you let your guard down."

That one sentence made Leo think of his dad. That's exactly what happened. He was helping someone and let his guard down. For the first time since the accident, Leo smiled about it. His dad had been such a loving man, right up until the end. "You're very smart about the water," Leo said with ease.

She nodded, taking his compliment quietly, then watched the ship travel out of sight, "Are you just saying that so I'll give you the group leader job?"

"No," he laughed. "But did I pass?"

"Yes, you passed. You have a group first thing in the morning. I noticed that you seem to be good with mature adults last Sunday when you took the group of young ladies to breakfast, so I have just the group for you: the Southern Magnolia Garden Club from Roswell, Georgia. If you're very good, maybe they'll take you to Sunrise for breakfast," she said and gave him a wink.

14

THE JOB OR THE GIRL

Trevor paced the bridge of the ship. "Port 10," he called out and watched the ship maneuver to his command. Looking ahead in the channel, he lined himself up for his next turn, then scanned his eyes across the marsh. This was always his and Maggie's favorite time of year when the marsh tried to hold on to its summer green but turned bright gold as it died out for the winter. Taking a deep breath, he said her name in a whisper, "Maggie."

How long had it been? He could barely remember. His long apprenticeship had become a blur, followed by the progression of licenses for different ton ships. Each one allowed him to handle larger vessels. But he was finally done. He no longer needed his dad's approval. He held his license from the state of Georgia; his dad could no longer place demands on him.

The first day he went into the crew as a regular licensed pilot was the day he went in search of Maggie. He had played out his forgiveness speech time after time. He knew it by heart. She was stubborn, so he knew it wouldn't be easy, but he wouldn't give up. She would eventually come around; he knew it in his heart. When he got to her house, her jeep was in the driveway, but she wasn't home. He waited for a few minutes, but then decided to grab a beer at AJs and give her time to get home.

When Trevor walked into the restaurant, the bartender recognized him and motioned him back to the deck where Maggie was sitting. As he rounded the corner, he saw Maggie, but she wasn't alone. She was sitting face to face with a dark-haired man. They were holding hands, and her eyes were closed as he talked into her ear.

Trevor saw red. "Who in the hell does he think he is?" he said under his breath as he began to approach them, but he stopped. *Who in the hell do I think I am?* he wondered. *I left her. This isn't the way to win her back.* He slowly backed away, without being seen, and walked to his truck.

Driving home, he thought back to the night his father had made him choose. "Every man has to make difficult choices, and here is yours. You can have this job or Maggie, but you can't have both. If you choose Maggie, I'm ending your apprenticeship. If you choose this job, you must break it off with Maggie, and she can't know it is by my request, or you will still lose your apprenticeship. No son of mine will ever marry anyone with the last name of Thomas."

"I don't understand, Dad. Where is all of this coming from? Aren't I doing really well on the river?"

"Yes, you're going to be an excellent pilot."

"And, don't you like Maggie? You've always gotten along so well with her."

"I do. I did. It doesn't matter. Those are my conditions.

You got this job because of me, and I can also take it away. One day you'll thank me for putting you out of your misery while you're still young."

Trevor balled his hands into fists so tight that his arms shook. He couldn't give Maggie up. He loved her. She was the best thing that had ever happened to him. He would figure this out; his dad was just being unreasonable. He took a deep breath and tried to talk this out. "What happened, Dad? This is crazy."

His dad cut him off. "My mind is made up. Let me know first thing in the morning what you decide," was all he said and then walked out the door.

Trevor had ridden around in his truck most of the night, and just as the sky began to show a tinge of light, he drove to Maggie's house. He made his decision. He was nothing without this job. She probably wouldn't even want him without this job. It was who he was, and he was good at it. What would he do without it? He knew nothing else. He made a plan. As soon as he was a licensed pilot and standing on his own, he would tell her everything. He knew she loved him; she wouldn't replace him.

Now he wasn't so sure. It had now been several weeks since the night he saw her at AJs, but he was still no closer to figuring out how to get her back. He took his buddy Jack to lunch to pick his brain, but Jack was closed up tighter than Fort Knox. Now, seeing her with the dark-haired man for a second time, he knew he must do something. Anything.

∾

WHEN MAGGIE GOT HOME that evening, she made a cup of hot tea and walked onto the back porch. The afternoon storm clouds were rolling in, and the sudden drop in temperature warned of imminent rain. She sat on the metal glider with the fluffy cushions, tucked her feet under her, and watched the sky. Something about storm clouds fascinated her, and living on the water afforded the perfect view.

It had been one heck of a day. Seeing Trevor on his way out of the port while they were at lunch and then coming back in on his second job when she was at the Cockspur Lighthouse, had shaken her. Even when they were a couple, she didn't see him that often. As if on cue, her phone rang. There was no use even checking; she knew it would be him.

She answered, expecting him to correct her for being in the wrong spot on the river. She kept waiting for his reprimand, but it never came. He asked about her day and how each of her friends was doing. They talked about how pretty it was on the water that afternoon now that the Indian Summer had changed the marsh from greens to golds. They had always enjoyed this time of year when they had been together.

Just as she asked Trevor why he was calling, Leo walked up in the backyard. After noticing her sitting on the porch, he bounded up the stairs and mouthed, "Do you have sugar?"

"Yes, it's in the pantry; help yourself," she had answered quietly, holding her hand over the phone.

"Do you have someone at your house?" Trevor asked.

"As a matter of fact, I do."

"Okay, Mags. I get it. We're not together right now. But do

you think I could take you to dinner tomorrow night so we can talk?" Trevor had asked.

Leo was standing in the doorway, and his presence gave her courage. She answered into the phone, "I think that six years gave us plenty of time to talk. If you couldn't say what you needed to during that time, then you never will. I see no need for us to communicate any further. Goodbye, Trevor." She walked past Leo in the doorway, went to the refrigerator, pulled out a lime, and sliced it. Then she pulled down the bottle of tequila and the saltshaker. She licked the salt from her hand, threw back the shot of tequila, and bit into the tart lime.

Leo laughed, "That must have been one hell of a phone call, but no one should drink alone." He followed the steps she had just completed and turned up the shot of tequila, and slammed down the glass. Choking through his words, he asked, "You want to talk about it?"

She nodded, so Leo picked up the bottle of tequila. She put her hand on top of the bottle and shook her head no, then poured them both a glass of lemonade and walked back out to the porch. She started at the beginning of her tale as tiny pellets of rain pinged onto the tin roof. Joe came running onto the porch beating the rain by seconds. He jumped up next to her, started pawing the fluffy pillows, and settled in a ball next to Maggie. Her hand stroked the top of his head. Every time she got to a sad part of the story, she started crying. Leo continually handed her tissues from the dispenser decorated with shell art that she had made for her grandmother as a girl.

When her story ended, Leo turned the tissue dispenser in each direction, studying the ugly box. "What...exactly...is this?" She was finally able to swallow her sobs as she laughed through her tears. Then he continued, "I really hate to say this, but Trevor might not be such a bad guy. Maybe he's just not the right guy for you. He probably did you a favor by letting you go, and you probably deep down know that because now you can get on with your life."

Their eyes locked for a long moment, then Maggie took a deep breath in and sighed as she exhaled. She had never looked at it like that. She had selfishly thought that she had invested six years of her life with him and that she deserved to be married in the end. She wondered why Trevor didn't feel like she was good enough to marry, but what if he truly wasn't the man God had meant for her to share the rest of her life with?

Leo jumped up, "Sugar! Aunt Regina sent me to get sugar for her baking. I'm going to be in trouble with her." Then he paused, walked over to Maggie, and gently pushed back a piece of hair that had fallen in her eyes. "Are you okay? I can come right back if you want me to."

She stood up, wrapped her arms around his neck, and gave him a light kiss on the cheek. "I feel better now than I have in a very long time. I'm gonna take a long bath and hit the sack. Thank you for listening."

He kissed her forehead and wagged his eyebrows at her. "You're going to take a hot bath and hit the sack? Do you need any help with that?" She swatted at him, and he ran out the porch door with sugar in tow. The smell of his cologne lingered on her shirt, and she hugged it tight to her chest and grinned. Leo had made her feel so much better. She said a quick prayer of thanksgiving that God had brought him back to Savannah, at least for the time being.

15

THE LOVE OF A FATHER

Venice, Italy

Pietro was a quiet man. He loved art and music and was more comfortable surrounded by paintings and symphonies than speaking with other human beings. He was shocked when Monica Rossi showed interest in him. She was beautiful, and while he lacked gumption, she had it ten-fold. They were married in San Moisè one year to the day of their first meeting. At that time, his father was the premiere gondolier for the Biancos, so they had the grandest wedding of the season.

Pietro was very good at what he did; his father had taught him everything he knew. However, his training wasn't complete. The morning after his father died in his sleep, Pietro was left without a license. Therefore, the job was given to someone else, his father's brother, Claudio Vianello. Monica had barely left her bedroom for three weeks following the funeral. All of Venice knew about the privileges the Vianellos had enjoyed; she had expected that she would one day reap those benefits.

Pietro had not been upset to have missed the chance at this privileged position. His father had never been home, and he didn't want that for his family. He still became a gondolier, but enjoyed working four to five days a week instead of being available 24 hours a day for the Bianco family. Pietro's shuttling of visitors from the many tourist spots gave him time to do what he loved. After a few years, he finally talked Monica into having a baby. Some women glow while pregnant, but Monica wore a constant scowl. Mita helped her along with her various herbs. Still, she hated how pregnancy changed her body and vowed that this one child would be her last. That was one vow she had actually kept.

The day Michael was born was the second happiest day of Pietro's life. The father and son were inseparable. But after Claudio's untimely death, Pietro found himself away from home most of the time. He missed his old life, but he missed his time with Michael most of all. When he was given a day off, he planned to spend that day with his son.

Pietro and Michael made their way through Campo Santa Margherita. They talked comfortably about Michael's friends, who attended the neighboring universities, and then planned where they would eat lunch on their way home. They shared a love for art, and much of Michael's childhood had been spent in the many museums around Venice. Their favorite was the Peggy Guggenheim Museum. They had been museum members for as long as he could remember and were invited to every private event. That day, they would be viewing the Picasso Black and White exhibition.

Upon entering the museum, Pietro let out a long sigh. "I haven't been here in over a year. I used to come at least once a week, whether for one hour or ten. Oh, how I've missed it."

They learned from the many plaques that hung on the entryway walls that Peggy Guggenheim was the daughter of the wealthy New York businessman, Benjamin Guggenheim, who went down on the Titanic in 1912. She had purchased the house on Canal Grande in 1949 and made it the home for her art collection. She loved Venice and gave herself to the city, who returned the affection by crowning her an honorary citizen. They called her "L'ultima Dogaressa," meaning 'the last female duke.' A few years before her death, she transferred ownership of the collection to her family in New York, The Solomon R. Guggenheim Foundation.

Family stories always fascinated Michael, but it made him sad that he was an only child of two only children. He treasured his time with his sweet aunt Mita, but as he got older he saw her less and less. He often wondered how different his life would have been if he had a large family.

After winding their way through the many rooms, they came to the featured exhibit. He and his father tackled it as usual. They made one quick sweep, then went back and pondered each piece, discussing it before moving to the next. When they finally exited the building, they compared what they considered their "favorite" and chuckled at each other's answers. They stopped for a slice of pizza on their way home, then Pietro took Michael for gelato just like he did when he was a boy. As they sat on a bench along the side of the Campo, Michael started the conversation.

"Are you happy, Papa? Is working for the Biancos everything you ever thought it would be?"

Pietro pondered the question for a long time, so long that Michael wondered if he had asked the question out loud. Then his dad ruffled Michael's hair like he had when he was a child and answered, "You are a good boy to worry about your papa. I often ask myself what pleasing things I've done in God's eyes that He has blessed me with such a good boy. It is an honor and privilege to have the job I do, and every gondolier would love to be in my shoes. But to me, it's only a job. What makes me happy is you and your mama. So, to answer your question, yes, I'm very happy, but it's not because of my job."

Michael acknowledged what his dad had said, but asked one final question. "What if the job with the Biancos had never come available?"

"As I said, it's just a job. I would be equally as happy." Then he nudged Michael with his elbow, adding, "We would have seen many more exhibits this year though, wouldn't we?" They stood and began to walk when Pietro stopped abruptly at the first stall in the outdoor market. It was full of all types of flowers, but he chose a large bouquet of wildflowers. "But I couldn't give your mama all the flowers and trinkets that she requires," he said as he winked at his son, and they made their way home.

MICHAEL WALKED out of the confessional and towards the pew in front of the statue of the Virgin Mary. He always came to this spot to do his penance, and the familiarity of it brought him comfort. He had asked for forgiveness again, although he had already confessed the offense twice. He understood that his sin had been absolved, but his conscience still felt the burden.

As he bowed his head, he began the Apostles Creed and steadily made his way through the Luminous Mysteries, the penance the priest had given him. When he began the final prayer, Hail Holy Queen, he looked at the statue of Jesus' mother and prayed:

"Pray for us, O holy Mother of God

That we may be made worthy of the promises of Christ."

The words "that we may be made worthy" saddened him. How could he be made worthy? He bowed his head and thought about his dad and their conversation as they had walked home from the exhibit. Could his father have been happy if he hadn't become the Biancos' gondolier?

But what about his mother? Could she be happy if her husband no longer worked for the Biancos? He closed his eyes and pictured himself sitting at the kitchen table, agreeing to sway the truth. He could still hear the sound of her heels clicking away from him on the hardwood floors. But upon opening his eyes, he realized it was the sound of another person's heeled shoes on the church's marble floors, and they had stopped right behind him. Suddenly he felt a hand upon his shoulder. When he turned, he was staring into the eyes of Claudio's widow. Just like her late husband's eyes, they were full of kindness, vastly different from the cold eyes of his mother.

She leaned over and asked him in her best Italian whisper, which wasn't much like a whisper, "May I speak with you when you are finished?" He nodded to her then focused on the crucifix hanging about the main altar.

"Jesus, I trust in You!" he said to himself, the same way he ended all his prayers. Then he made the Sign of the Cross, got up from the kneeler, and offered his elbow to her as they walked out the side door of Chiesa di San Martino church. Even before his eyes adjusted to the bright light, Mrs. Vianello wrapped her arms around Michael and began to sob. Her grief paralyzed him initially, but he began to soothe her, patting her back until she quieted.

"I've been praying that I would one day run into you, but I don't make it to the city very often, especially now that Leo has left. It's fitting to find such a nice young man in the church," she said. He flinched both from her calling him "nice" and the news that Leo had left, and he hoped that she hadn't noticed. She continued. "You were the last person who held my Claudio, and I must know, do you think that he suffered?" She barely finished her sentence before the sobs returned. Michael led her to a nearby bench, and she grabbed his hand and held it tightly.

"By the time I got to him," he paused, recognizing the weight his words held, and then continued, "he was already gone." She wailed so loudly that the people passing by began to stare, but he didn't care. Comforting Claudio's widow was the first noble thing he had done for his family, so he finished, "Your husband was a true hero. He did something most men would never do; he gave his life for the life of a stranger. Surely, God has rewarded him for it. I know nothing can soften the pain of your loss, but it happened quickly. He died instantly."

Mrs. Vianello sat up a little straighter, wiped under her

eyes, and put her handkerchief into her purse. She gave one nod and stood up. "Thank you for your honesty, Michael. Your words have given me much comfort. I know your mom must be proud to have you for her son." Then she kissed both of his cheeks.

He watched her figure grow smaller and smaller as she traveled down the sidewalk along the canal. He shook his head and grumbled, "My mom is very proud, but she's proud of my dis-honesty."

16

THE RETREAT

Tybee Island, Georgia

The group met early Friday morning at Tybee's Back River ramp. When the diocesan event planner called Maggie in April to schedule the weekend outing, she thought it was a great idea, but now she questioned herself. October usually remained warm, but there had been a steady drop all week, and it wasn't scheduled to get past 55 degrees all weekend. She was grateful the water temperature remained warmer.

She'd seen ads for the marriage retreat over several weeks in her church bulletin and around town. The retreat was led by Father Sullivan, who Maggie knew well from her time at Saint Vincent's Academy and a husband and wife who handled the marriage preparations for the Diocese of Savannah. The group would consist of seven couples from across the diocese who had been married for five years or less.

Maggie gave a short demonstration on handling the kayak and paddling, then they shoved off. The group, including Maggie and Leo, paddled for about an hour, took a break at a spot with a sandy shore inside Jack's Cut, then paddled about an hour more to the island. Once again, Maggie had sent supplies over earlier with Mac. She and Leo spent the better portion of the morning helping the group.

As the couples set up their tents, Maggie remembered Father Sullivan had added two couples at the last minute but she had forgotten to add their tents. She and Leo would be required to sleep under the large tarp they had strung between various trees for a covered meeting space. At lunch, everyone enjoyed the sandwiches Maggie had made the night before, and by 2:00, they started the program.

Father Sullivan had made a makeshift altar out of driftwood, and they had Mass on the beach. Maggie had never been to an outdoor Mass before and was unprepared when her senses became ultra-heightened as the priest consecrated the host outside. She was embarrassed when a sigh escaped her mouth, but was happy when Leo looked at her and nodded with a smile.

After Mass, Father Sullivan asked to speak with Maggie and Leo. "We had two couples register at the last minute and really need an even number of couples. Would you consider being part of the group whenever possible?"

"Oh, we aren't married, Father," Maggie explained to the priest.

"No one knows that; they just see that you are a couple. It would be doing me a great favor," Father Sullivan emphasized and winked at Maggie.

Maggie's eyes widened, thinking back to the night at the

police station when Father Sullivan had done her a great favor. He had been sitting in the station with an older gentleman the night the police brought her in after the Friday night high school football game.

"The Circle" was a vacant lot set about a half-mile off Benedictine's campus. It was well known for its proximity to the high school being far enough away to fight without being expelled. But on weekend nights, it became the hot spot to socialize. With several past graduates on the force, the local police knew the location well and always kept things in order.

That night, her friends were divided into two cars; Agnes drove one car while Jan drove the other. When the police came, the teens scattered. Both Agnes and Jan thought Maggie was with the other. When The Circle emptied, she was left standing in the parking lot alone, holding a Coors Light she had barely taken a sip of.

Father Sullivan persuaded the officers to release Maggie, but she had been upset afterward. He had told her, "Please don't worry, Maggie. Only God knows the day that I might need your help in return." She had smiled at that time, wondering how she could ever help a man of God, but now she knew.

Maggie answered before Leo could tell the priest that they weren't even a couple. "Sure, we would love to." Leo gave her a questioning look, but after the priest walked off, she simply said, "This will be fun."

There was only one presentation that afternoon. It was about each person's family of origin, and how values and traditions are usually brought from the families you grow up in. After the presentation was over, they broke into small groups. Leo and Maggie had been paired with Robert and Sheri, and they hit it off immediately. They slowly went through the small group questions; the last question was about traditions. Leo was the last in the group to explain his family's traditions. The other couples in the neighboring small groups finished and slowly drifted over to theirs, as did Father Sullivan and the Dowlings.

Leo told stories of Sant' Erasmus at Christmas and going to Midnight Mass in Venice at Saint Mark's on Christmas Eve to meet his dad, who always worked that afternoon. He also shared about his home parish, Cristo Rey. He told stories of Carnivale and the two-week celebration ending on Shrove Tuesday, which was their Fat Tuesday. Of course, his favorite part of the celebration was the Water Parade. Then he explained Saint Mark's Day when Venice celebrates its patron saint. On that day of many festivities, there was a gondolier regatta, but his favorite part was Bocolo Fest, when a man gives a red rose to the woman he loves. He always remembered his dad giving a rose to his mom. Leo had been deep in his thoughts, and when he looked up, he noticed everyone listening. "I can't wait to be able to give a rose to Maggie one day."

Maggie realized that her head had fallen to the side and her mouth was gaping open when all the women around them sighed in unison, "Ahhhhh!" Leo glanced over at Maggie and winked, snapping her back to reality. She knew that he was only acting and they weren't a couple but was there more? Robert gave Leo a very firm handshake as he left the group. He told Leo that he and Sheri always wanted to go to Venice, and Leo's story just sealed the deal.

The weekend had been chilly, but not uncomfortable. However, once the rain started after dinner on Saturday night, the temperature started dropping. Maggie was thankful that it had held out until they had finished the program for the day. As the couples scurried off from dinner under the tarp to the safety of their tents, Leo and Maggie cleaned up and then settled in.

"I actually learned a lot today," Leo said.

"Like what?" Maggie asked in return.

"Well, I loved the segment about communication with your spouse and how it runs through every area of your life. Family, friends, business partners, and couples should have mutual respect. Without respect, it's hard to continue in a healthy relationship." As he said that, his mind wandered to his fellow gondoliers in Venice, but he shook it away quickly. "I also loved the segment on spirituality. The goal, as a couple, is to be in union with God in our daily life, and it's our job to help get our spouse into heaven. That one is crazy to think about and will be a tough job for my wife." He paused, searching her eyes. "How do you feel about that?"

Maggie wanted to ask him where she could apply for the job, but quickly agreed. "I think your wife will be a very busy lady." She held his stare for what seemed like an eternity and was startled when her two-way radio started going off.

Mac wanted to give them a heads up that a storm system was coming through during the night and told her he would be there first thing in the morning. She put Leo in charge of pulling the kayaks high on the beach and securing the coolers and loose items around the tarp area. At the same time, Maggie made her rounds securing the tents. She let Father Sullivan know what was coming and then went back to try to get some sleep before it hit.

The wind picked up around 3:00 a.m. Since Maggie and Leo were sleeping under a tarp without sides, they got soaked. They huddled close together and put their waterproof sleeping bags over their heads as the wind knocked them side to side. Maggie heard herself cry out just one time, but Leo pulled her close into his chest, and she was able to relax.

Maggie woke at first light, propped against a bag of life jackets and lying on Leo's chest. She glanced up to see him looking at the sky while he held her. He noticed her moving and said, "It might have taken a storm to get you in my arms but be careful, I could get used to this."

She smiled at him as he pointed up. Her eyes followed to a corner of the tarp that had fallen down during the night. It had been tied to a palm tree, but she noticed the palm was deformed when she looked up. It had grown halfway up then divided into two crowns. When she squinted her eyes, the light coming in between the crowns made the shape of a heart.

"I've never in my life seen a palm tree with two tops. It's amazing," she said.

"Yes, it is. Funny that it's in the shape of a heart, too." He leaned over and gave her a soft kiss on the lips, then stood and helped her onto her feet. They looked around at the mess the storm had made with seaweed and palm fronds scattered everywhere, but all the tents had thankfully withheld the storm. Leo made himself busy by picking up, while Maggie began cooking the big breakfast she always offered on the last morning. She was so happy she had covered the firewood the night before.

As always, as soon as the smell of coffee and bacon hit the air, the couples staggered out of their tents. Some had slept through the storm, and some had been very worried they wouldn't make it through, but each had their own rendition of the tale. She knew the couples would never forget this retreat, and the tall tale of the storm on the final night would make it even more memorable.

After breakfast, the group finished the retreat talking about marital intimacy. Maggie was uncomfortable with the presentation about romance, but she was fascinated with the discussion on natural family planning. She wondered how she had been raised Catholic and never taught about this scientific way to plan the size of families by identifying ovulation.

The retreat ended with a "Go Forth" Mass. Father Sullivan stated that love was not merely a feeling in his homily. Feelings can come and go. In strong marriages, spouses live out the promises made on their wedding day to put each other first. Maggie knew that her heart was truly ready for marriage whenever God brought her the right spouse. She secretly wondered if it could be Leo.

17

LEAVING TOWN

While Maggie, Mac, and Leo put things away back at LRS headquarters, Leo was unusually quiet. Mac had asked Maggie if anything had happened on the trip and she assured him that Leo had been great. As they finished, Leo told them he needed to get home and check on his aunt, and left quickly.

"Okay, spill. What happened between the two of you?" Mac asked.

"Absolutely nothing, I promise. Well, except, maybe it could be that we had to act like we were married. Father Sullivan asked us to sit in on the retreat," she answered.

"Yep, that would do it," Mac replied.

"But nothing happened, Mac. Leo said he really enjoyed it." Mac gave her a sideways glance, so she quickly added. "Okay, I'll go talk to him later and see if everything's kosher." But later, when she walked to his house, his aunt said that he had gone to town, and the following morning his car was gone before dawn.

That weekend had been the last adventure trip on her books until the following March, and she had informed her staff that they would close for a few weeks, so she had spent most of the following week finishing up the books. Mac closed up the building and stored the kayaks. The weather in Savannah rarely got into the thirties, so there wasn't any winterizing to be done.

Maggie thought it was odd that she hadn't seen Leo all week, and wondered if he had found another job. That thought alone put her in a rotten mood.

When she got home on Thursday, she made herself a sandwich, grabbed one of the many books she was reading, and moved to an Adirondack chair down on the bluff over-looking the river. She had just taken the first bite of her sandwich when she felt a hand rub across her hair.

"*Ciao, bella.*"

"Leo!" she exclaimed with far too much excitement. She watched a small piece of her chewed sandwich fly out of her mouth. She put her fingers to her lips, hoping there was no food left hanging. "I'm so happy to see you!" She realized just how much she had missed him. He took a seat in the matching Adirondack and asked for the other half of the sandwich. She handed it to him timidly, inspecting it for stray crumbs. "Can I speak to you for a minute?" he asked.

"Sure," she said enthusiastically.

"I think it's time for me to go."

"You just got here."

"No, I think it's time for me to go back to Sant' Erasmus."

Her heart gripped tight. All she could say was, "Oh."

"I want you to go with me," he suggested.

"Go with you?"

"Let me explain. I realized this past weekend at the retreat that it was time to go home. You see, I've been running. Actually, I've been running for a long time and I can't really start living until I make some decisions. I'm not sure that I want to be a gondolier anymore." He gave a long exhale. "Whew, I can't believe I just admitted that. My dad and I were very close. We had a special connection. We both were gondoliers. We had a job in the city where the rest of my family were on Sant' Erasmus. I spent more time with my dad than anyone else, and his death left a huge void in my life. Since his death a year ago, I have been so unhappy, until I came to Savannah and found you again. The last few months have been some of the happiest of my life. I love kayaking and I love being around people and guiding groups. I've been wondering if I could lead kayak tours in Venice."

Maggie listened, without interrupting. Leo continued, "You've done this before. You saved a business and have figured out what people want. Could you come to Venice, while Lazaretto River Sports is closed this winter, and help me?"

Maggie didn't realize she was shaking her head as she slowly processed the reasons she couldn't go to Venice. Taking a deep breath, she explained, "I'm the type of person that automatically says no to something without thinking it through. Can I please pray on this and let you know?"

Leo pulled her in for a hug, and then kissed her on the cheek. "Absolutely. I'm not going to pressure you, but please let me know in the next couple of days so that we can order plane tickets." He hesitated, then added, "There's more. I didn't want to cloudy the water before asking you." He sheepishly looked out at the water, then back to her. "I think there may be more between us. I know you feel it, too. The only reason I didn't want to leave Tybee was because I didn't want to leave you. I hope we can spend more time together in Italy."

Maggie felt the tug on her heart. He leaned over and kissed her once, very softly. Then he stood up, took her hand, raised her so she was standing, and took her in his arms. The second kiss told it all. It was intense and held a promise of many kisses to come in their future, a future that she had waited so long to find.

IT WAS AGNES' turn to choose the lunch spot and she chose Miyabi. They sat around the large grill service and placed their order. When the chef came, pushing his cart with the raw food, he called them all by name. They all gave each other confused looks; they didn't recognize him. He was a big guy with glasses who stood at least 6'2". The tall chef's hat pushed him closer to seven feet and made him look like a giant. Someone had drawn black eyeliner slits on his eyes to give him the appearance of being Asian, but the make-up had become smudged by the heat of the grill.

He focused on Agnes, prompting the group to look quizzically at one another, desperate to figure out his identity. He stayed busy with his work and asked questions to the group about their marriage status and which ones were in serious relationships.

Although the food was delicious, he wasn't very good at doing the tricks that the tableside chefs were known for at Miyabi. The chefs usually cut the tails off the shrimp and toss them into the top of their hats, but as this chef tossed, one landed in Latrice's drink. Then, when it was time to spin the salt shaker, his quick glance at Agnes made him lose focus and the salt shaker flew past Jan's head and hit the wall with a bam. He was so distracted that once all the food was on their plates, he excused himself while a young waitress finished and cleaned up.

It had been such an interesting show that no one had dared interrupt with their usual chatter. After the center grill was turned off, Maggie began, "I've got some news. Leo is going back to Italy."

They all chimed in, "Ah, Im sorry," and, "Dang, are you alright?"

Maggie stopped them by holding up her hand, "And he asked me to go with him."

They were all eagerly waiting for her to continue, when the waitress asked if there was a Miss Agnes at their table. Agnes raised her hand like a school kid answering a question. She was directed to follow the waitress and was told that the owner wished to speak with her. Agnes looked at her friends, who all shrugged, before she stood up and walked down the hall.

"Okay, tell us everything, Maggie," Kathleen said.

Maggie told them the whole story beginning with the retreat, Father Sullivan asking for the return favor for the event which they all remembered like yesterday, and ending with Leo admitting he had feelings for her and the kiss.

They were all listening to her with sweet smiles on their faces, and the picture made Maggie laugh out loud.

"How long would you be going for?" Stephanie asked.

"I'd be home by the last week in February to get ready for LRS to open in March," she answered.

"Damn, Maggie. That's fourteen weeks. Have you ever been away from home for fourteen weeks straight?" asked Latrice.

"No, but honestly I need a break. It's been a heck-of-a long summer and fall. I'm seriously considering going," she answered.

Just at that time, Agnes came back to the table escorted by a tall and handsome man. She had laced her hand inside the elbow bend of his custom-made suit. Agnes introduced him, "I think ya'll remember Bradley." Bradley was Agnes' boyfriend of three years from Notre Dame who had spent many weeks of his summers with Agnes in Savannah. When they graduated from college, Agnes came home while Bradley moved to Boston.

"Hello ladies," he said. They all looked at each other with confused expressions, and he continued. "It was a pleasure serving you all today." They erupted in laughter together, as he continued. "I saw Agnes walk in and I hatched my crazy plan to find out if she was married, so I grabbed the chef's hat and glasses and came to you. I haven't cooked in ten years. Sorry I was so out of practice. The owner of a food chain seldom gets to have the fun of cooking the food. The meals are on the house." As he started to leave, he added, "I hope to see a lot more of you all while I'm in town." Then he turned to Agnes and added, "Especially you."

She gave him a little curtsy, and as he walked away the girls started hooting and laughing. They said their goodbyes in the parking lot, telling Maggie to please let them know as soon as she made her decision. Maggie hugged each of their necks a little longer than usual, just in case she wouldn't see them for fourteen weeks, knowing she must decide soon.

18

THE PILOT'S PLEA

Trevor walked down the front steps of his downtown Savannah townhome. He had only lived there a few months and was still getting accustomed to living in the city. Glancing over to the adjacent square, he made eye contact with a neighbor walking his dog. They both nodded in acknowledgment and went about their business.

As he reached the waiting taxi, he threw his work bag in the backseat and began to climb in when someone called his name.

"Heading to work?" Jack asked, expecting Trevor would most likely be taking a taxi to be dropped off at a ship.

Trevor stepped from the cab to shake Jack's hand. "You know it. Day and night, the ships never sleep, thank heavens." Trevor motioned to Jack's briefcase. "Burning the midnight oil?"

"Yes. Kathleen's going to kill me for missing dinner." He

motioned at the night sky, "and night prayers and bedtime. But I've got a big case and couldn't get away."

"How's everybody doing?" Trevor asked. "How's Maggie?"

Jack paused, wondering if he should share the news. "She's fine. She's actually going to Italy."

Trevor pulled back, visibly upset. Briefly closing his eyes, he shook his head, picturing the dark-haired man. "When?"

"Well, I'm not one hundred percent sure, but I think she may be leaving in a couple of days."

Trevor looked down at his watch. "I gotta go, Jack. I have a twenty-one hundred in-bound. Give my love to Kathleen and the kiddos," he called out over his shoulder, climbed in the taxi, and was gone.

TREVOR LOOKED out the window of the taxi, watching the stretches of marsh fly by as he rode to the pilot base on Cockspur Island. He believed Maggie would wait for him. How could this be happening? Walking down the dock, he climbed onto the waiting pilot boat, *The Georgia*. The boat would first collect another pilot who was taking a tanker out of port; then, Trevor would be delivered to his ship coming into the harbor. He pulled his phone from his pocket and began to scroll through pictures to pass the time.

Trevor glanced up, feeling the bump as the pilot boat maneuvered alongside the ship. As always, the boat had positioned itself steadily with the moving ship and waited in place as the pilot expertly climbed down the hanging ladder and stepped onto the platform on the pilot boat. Trevor let out a loud groan when he saw that the pilot was his father.

James entered the cabin, letting his eyes adjust to the red light inside. "Hello, Trevor," he said as he walked towards his son and offered two firm pats on his back. Looking down, James saw the picture of Maggie on Trevor's phone. "I thought you were over that one," he said, motioning to the phone. "You seem to always have a new girl on your arm."

Trevor couldn't control his anger and shot to his feet. "Don't you ever talk to me about Maggie again. You've done enough. She's leaving the country for a while and not going alone." A small smile crept across James' face.

Once again, the pilot boat made the familiar bump against the moving inbound ship, bringing Trevor back into the present moment. "Yeah, I'm sure that makes you happy. But the jokes on you. I'm gonna get her back, and there isn't a damn thing you can do about it anymore." He motioned toward the ship. "As soon as I'm off this monster, I'm going to tell her everything." He picked up his bag and walked past his father, making sure to bump him with his shoulder on the way out.

While James watched his son step from the moving pilot boat and onto the hanging pilot ladder, he searched for Maggie's address on his phone. James drove straight to Maggie's house as soon as the boat arrived back at Cockspur. He cursed his bad luck when she wasn't home, knowing he would need to go to Lazaretto, something he had promised himself never todo again.

He turned off Highway 80 and onto the long crush-and-run road that snaked under the bridge and led to several waterfront businesses. Lazaretto River Sports was the first and sat far away from the others. James knew why the man-made trench encircled the large piece of property, but that was no longer his secret to bare.

Noticing Maggie's car parked in one of the spaces, he pulled his car beside hers and walked down the drive. His eyes were drawn past the office and down to the dock, where shadows caught his eye. The large oak trees over the marsh made the dusk of night darker than usual, and James squinted his eyes, trying to focus. The prickle of the hair on his arms warned him of what he already knew; the spirits were restless.

James hurried towards the office, hoping to hide from the wandering souls. He was relieved the front door was unlocked, so he walked inside. The door chimed as he entered, causing a voice to call out from somewhere down the hall, "I'm in my office. Come on back." James followed the hallway to the only room with the lights on. As he turned the corner, he looked to the girl who had captured his son's heart.

She was busy working and hadn't stopped to look up. Her long hair was hanging freely over the desk as she wrote. She was pretty. Well, obviously, she was pretty; she looked just like Victoria. He paused for a second. He could turn around and not put this ball into motion. But then he thought about Alex at the poker game and his own promise to rid his family of them. Clearing his throat, he said, "Hello, Maggie."

His deep and raspy voice startled her, causing her to jump. Confused, she looked at him and then glanced past him like she was expecting someone else. Finally, she answered, "Hello," then added, "How are you?"

"Fine, fine," he said quickly as he surveyed the room. "The office looks a helluva lot better than when I owned it." He looked at her and smiled when Maggie finally realized what he had just said. "Didn't you know I owned this building before you?" She shook her head no, and he gladly explained. "Yeah, your tricky father won it from me in a poker game."

Maggie sat very still, replaying the conversation she and her father had when he gave her the business. He had conveniently left out the name of the prior owner. She pulled herself together, looked James in the eyes, and said, "My father is good at many things. I wish I could tell you I'm sorry that you lost, but I sure do love my business."

Her statement aggravated James. She wasn't a thing like her mother: sweet and proper. She had too much of her dad's straggly blood running through her. James proceeded to bait her. "I was so upset after the game, I drove straight to Trevor's house and told him that I wasn't allowing my son to marry a cheater's daughter."

Maggie's mind was reeling. Trevor wouldn't do that. But then she thought about the abruptness of their break-up, and all the pieces fell into place. He left her at his father's request. Her eyes began to sting, but she wouldn't allow tears to leak out. "Why are you here?" she asked.

"I just saw the light on when I drove over the bridge and wanted to drop by to say hello." James turned to leave, but stopped in the doorway. "Please send my love to Victoria," he said with a smile and walked out the front door.

Maggie sat at her desk for a long time, trying to accept the many lies that surrounded her. She was startled when her phone buzzed from a text message. Glancing down, she noticed that it was from Trevor.

"Maggie. I need to talk with you, but I'm on a ship. Could you meet me for an early breakfast?"

She typed a long and hateful text, but deleted it. She had to know the truth, and Trevor held all the answers. She sent a simple text, "Eggcelent Cafe at 7." She threw the phone down, not waiting for a reply.

Shaking her head, she stood up and began pacing the small office. "I've got to get out of this town," she muttered to herself. Then she picked up the phone and sent an all-caps message to Leo. "I WOULD LOVE TO GO TO VENICE WITH YOU!"

TREVOR WAS SITTING at a table when she arrived. He stood and started towards her for a hug, but she sat quickly. Before the waitress came to the table, she blurted out. "Your father paid me a visit last night." She watched the shock in his face and almost felt sorry for him. Almost.

He immediately started talking, quickly trying to explain himself. He jumped from the poker game to his father's demands. "He made me choose. I could continue my apprenticeship to become a pilot, or I could be with you," Trevor said as if that should explain everything, then paused to take a breath.

She took that opportunity to jump in. Leaning forward, she asked, "You chose a job over me?" He wouldn't meet her eyes, so she sat back and repeated it. But this time as a statement. "You chose a job over me, *and* you didn't have the guts or respect to tell me why."

Once again, he quickly tried to give another excuse about his father, but when Maggie stood up, he stopped talking. She leaned on the table and looked him in the eye, "What's done is done. You made a choice and got exactly what you wanted...your job. Goodbye, Trevor," she said and left him sitting at the table alone.

19

MADE FOR GREATNESS

Maggie didn't want to confront her father but knew that she must. Unfortunately, she would be forced to wait. Just like every other morning, the shrimp boat had pulled out at the first morning light. So she stayed busy around LRS, tying up loose ends and meeting with Mac to go over the billing and spring schedules. Mac's livelihood depended on the company, so she wanted to assure him that the business would continue to run in her absence.

Maggie was sitting at the kitchen table when Alex walked in. She could smell the all-too-familiar scent of shrimp before she saw him. She was in the middle of taking a bite of a frozen pinwheel cookie, which her father always kept a supply of stashed in the freezer, when he came around the corner. Taking in the scene of his daughter sitting at the table by herself eating his cookies made him stop. "How's it going, sweet pea?" he asked.

"Just dandy, Dad. I had an interesting visitor late last

night at the office; James. He had a lot to say about a poker game, my business, and, well, my life."

Her dad stood still for a brief moment, then sat down at the table beside her and told her his side of the story. He explained the night of the poker game, about James losing his kayak company and his threat to pluck Maggie from his family's life at the end of the game. "I had no idea what he was capable of. When I drove to your house and found you on the front porch, all I wanted to do was take care of you. That's what I've been trying to do since." He cleared his throat, then finished, "Can you forgive me?"

"You want my forgiveness? Do you have any idea the hell I've put myself through the last two years? Two years, Dad. You've had two years to tell me all of this." She shook her head in disbelief, but it quickly turned to anger. "I thought it was me. I thought I wasn't good enough for Trevor. But it had nothing to do with me. We were just chess pieces being played by two people who didn't give two shits about their children." She began to walk away and remembered her company. "The kayak company that you gave me belonged to Trevor's family. Are you kidding me? Do you know how twisted that is?"

"I know it sounds weird, but when you asked for it, I thought about how much had been taken from you and how it would only be fair to give you something in return. When I saw how happy it made you, I knew it had been the right thing to do."

"The right thing? Well, I don't want it. I don't want anything from you."

"It's yours now. You made it into the company it is. Do with it as you wish." He heard movement behind him and looked back to see Victoria standing in the doorway. She had listened to the whole story. She shook her head at him, turned, and walked away.

As he turned his attention back to Maggie, she said, "You were there for me every step of the way after Trevor left. I felt so lucky that my dad loved me so much. But now I see why you were there, and it had nothing to do with love. It was guilt." He reached his hand towards her, but she pulled away. "I've gotta go. I'm getting the hell out of this town. I'm going to Italy," she blurted out, "and I may never come back."

As she drove away, she glanced in her rearview mirror and saw him standing in the driveway. She felt a twinge of guilt for her meanness. There was a fine line between respecting your elders and calling them out on their mistakes. Maybe her time away in Venice would do them both some good.

MAGGIE TURNED OFF HER PHONE. She gave her full attention to closing up her house for the weeks ahead; her first endeavor was cleaning out the refrigerator. She studied the various magnets and pictures hanging from its front. It held everything from bottle openers and pizza delivery phone numbers to photos of the people she loved. As she opened the door, she wondered when the last time she had cleaned her refrigerator was. Then she remembered the hurricane evacuation three years back and the craziness of racing to get out of its path.

Every year, from June to November, residents in the Low Country kept their eyes on the National Weather broadcasts.

And almost every year, a monster of a storm caused the residents in that area to evacuate inland. That particular storm had knocked the power out for a week, and Maggie had come home to a refrigerator full of sour sauces and dressings. She cringed, thinking of the smell that lingered in her house, and quickly began to pull all of the half-empty bottles out.

She walked around the house, tidying and picking up; ran a load of dishes; and finished washing her clothes. By the time her suitcase was packed, darkness had settled in. She pulled out the box of her secret stash, Fruity Pebbles, and poured herself a bowl. Using the very last of her gallon of milk, she took her dinner out on the back porch.

As she ate, Joe came and wrapped himself around her feet. For whatever reason, his furry presence put a lump in her throat as she thought of not seeing her faithful companion for so many weeks. Once the sadness started, it snowballed, quickly followed by doubt.

She ran her hands across the pillows on the outdoor couch. After so much time, she could still picture Trevor laying back on them with his hands crossed behind his head, telling her how much he loved her and talking about their future together. She had spent six years with him. How had he thrown her away so easily? And for what, a job? Now she knew the reasons behind their abrupt end. She was mad at her dad, but a new ire burned in her belly for Trevor. She knew that he loved her, but he just didn't love her enough. He wanted the job so badly he chose to let her go.

She had so much new information she needed to process, but Leo would be picking her up at five a.m. the following day for their seven o'clock flight. She needed to get some sleep, so she went to bed. But going to bed and going to sleep are two very different things; her brain could not relax. She watched the clock all night, praying for a couple of hours of sleep. Her frustration increased every twenty minutes when she checked the time.

At 3:30, she gave up, threw off her covers, and walked into the kitchen. She felt the anxiety in her chest and the building cry lodged in her throat and prayed that she wouldn't have a full-blown panic attack. She felt it coming, so she started the deep belly breaths. Placing her hand on her abdomen, she said to herself, "Breathe in slow." She felt her stomach extend until she could no longer hold her breath in. "Exhale. Another one. Inhale." And as she did, she said through her O-shaped lips, "What am I doing?" And as she exhaled, she asked further, "Why am I going to Venice?"

She jumped when something knocked on her back door. Dizzy from her oxygen intake, she turned on the backdoor light. There was Leo. "You couldn't sleep either?" he asked and then noticed the worry between her eyes. "What's the matter, Maggie? What's got you so upset?"

She sat down at her grandmother's linoleum top kitchen table. She fiddled with the stretched-out neckline of her Guns' N Roses concert t-shirt. "I've found out some pretty crazy things in the last couple of days, and I'm so glad to be getting away. But I'm just scared. I can't explain it. I'm just comfortable here, and it's hard for me to leave."

Leo studied her wacky outfit. Maggie's T-shirt made her look like someone he wouldn't want to mess with, but the pink furry slippers said otherwise. Seeing how shaken up she was, he spoke quietly. "A great man once said, 'You were not made for comfort; you were made for greatness.' Don't let fear influence your life. I know it's easier said than done. But the word 'fear' is said so many times in the Bible for a reason. We are all scared, but that's not a reason to stop moving forward."

Maggie looked at him while reflecting on his words and slowly began to nod. "Who was the great man, Leo?"

"It was Pope Benedict XVI."

"Oh," Maggie said in a shaky voice, "then it must be true." She fiddled with a cigarette burn that was as old as the white speckled table. They sat in silence, but she glanced at the clock over the oven after several minutes. "It's 4:00. Time to get going, isn't it? Can I make you some coffee? I would offer breakfast, but I ate the last of it last night."

"Coffee would be great," Leo answered. And when Maggie stood up, Leo wrapped her in a bear hug and whispered in her ear. "You're gonna love Italy, you'll see."

20

WELCOME

L eo and Maggie watched a movie for the first hour of the long flight. However, the lack of sleep from the night before caught up with them both, and the plane's movement, along with two glasses of wine, lulled them to sleep. They leaned onto one another for comfort, but woke with a start when the plane landed at Marco Polo airport at 4:00 in the afternoon. They searched out the nearest coffee stand and then walked out of the terminal and down a covered path.

"How was your nap?" Leo asked.

"I don't remember the last time I slept that hard," she answered.

"Did you have nice dreams?" he prodded further, laughing when she eyed him suspiciously. "You know that you talk in your sleep, don't you?"

"I do not!" She giggled nervously while trying to recall what she had been dreaming about, worried that it might have included Leo.

"I wouldn't really call it 'talking' in your sleep. It was somewhere between a snore and a snort."

She swatted at him playfully, "You're messing with me, aren't you?"

"I don't know, am I?" he teased one last time as they reached the dock where Leo had arranged for his brother, Davide, to pick them up by boat. Once they started moving, the cold wind cut through her jacket. She couldn't remember a time when she was as cold as she was at that moment. She wanted to linger, admiring Venice in the distance. Nevertheless, she followed Davide's directions as he hurried her along towards a small cockpit covered with boxes of various vegetables and a small stool sitting in their center.

She smiled as she listened to Davide talking loudly over the boat's motor and to Leo talking fast in Italian. When she looked up through the doorway, she watched in amusement as their hands stayed in mid-air as they spoke. She had never seen Leo speak with his whole body before, and she found it incredibly attractive. She wondered what they were talking about so passionately.

When the boat slowed, she popped up to see the trees of Sant' Erasmus Island coming into view. Their boat moved past the docks and around a buoy, then slowed into a small canal. Unlike the creeks in the Low Country, the sides of the canal were moored with long planks. Maggie asked Leo if Sant' Erasmus had canals like Venice. He explained that they were similar and ran through the marshland and countryside.

They traveled a few more minutes, then Davide docked the boat and tied it off. Maggie stepped onto a small landing with a shelled path that led to a large two-story house. There were fields as far as the eye could see when she looked in the opposite direction.

"It's so beautiful here," Maggie said excitedly.

Leo grabbed the luggage and led the way down the path to the house. As they approached, Maggie realized the path continued past his house, and Leo explained it led to the main road. They walked into a courtyard area and under a trellis with the green remains of a wisteria vine. As soon as Leo opened the door, the wonderful aroma of sauces and bread caused Maggie's mouth to water. Leo's mom was standing at the stove cooking, but the second she saw Leo, she set the large wooden spoon beside the bubbling pot of sauce and ran to her son.

"*Il mio ragazzo,* I'm so glad you're home," she exclaimed as she kissed both his cheeks and ran her hand across his face. She then turned to Maggie. "*Ciao*, Maggie," she said as she looked her over from head to toe. She reached out and pushed a blonde curl that had fallen into Maggie's eyes. "When Leo said he was bringing you home to help him with something, I pictured the ten-year-old girl that lived next door to Regina, but look at you. Now I know why my Leo stayed gone for so long." She tenderly patted Maggie's cheek. "Please, make yourself at home, Maggie."

Maggie felt welcomed immediately and wondered why her heart never felt that way in her childhood home. Maggie was shown to a tiny room upstairs where she would be staying. She quickly put away her suitcase, hung her coat, and went back downstairs for dinner.

The kitchen had a large farmhouse table with many mismatched chairs, as well as several smaller tables pulled into the room. As they prayed before the meal, Maggie looked around the room and counted fifteen people. Leo's family included his brother, Davide, two sisters and their husbands, and many children. Some older teenagers worked on the farm, two children were school-age, and a toddler banged on his highchair with a spoon. The scene held so much love, and Maggie felt honored to be a part of it.

After the blessing, the women stood up and walked to the kitchen. Confused, Maggie looked at Leo, and he motioned his head in that direction. Mrs. Vianello handed each girl a dish of something, and they carried it to the table. Once everyone was seated, the food was passed around. Maggie watched how smoothly everyone took a portion and handed it to the next person. She followed their example. When the teenage girl shoved a fish dish in front of her, she let out a small yelp. The bug-eyed fish staring up at her was not what she was accustomed to. She took a small portion and passed it quickly, trying to keep up the group's pace. Once the last dish had made its rounds, she looked at her plate, laughed out loud, and said, "I've got enough food on my plate to feed a family."

Mrs. Vianello seemed pleased with that comment and said, "Good girl! Enjoy!"

Enjoy she did, every bite that went in her mouth. Pasta, sauces, seafood, meats, vegetables, and the bread were all to die for. When she forced the last bite into her mouth, she moaned aloud and sat back with a happy smile on her face. She looked over at Leo and said, "I love your family," and everyone laughed at her.

Leo excused himself and came back with small presents that Maggie had helped pick out for everyone before leaving the States. He had giant Hershey bars, pooka bead neck-laces, T-shirts, and sweatshirts that said Tybee Island, Georgia. He had pop guns for the boys and a little stuffed dolphin for the toddler. Then he pulled his mama aside and gave her a beautiful set of rosary beads he had purchased from Saints and Shamrocks, the unique Catholic bookstore in down-town Savannah.

Everyone enjoyed their gifts and hung around the table, talking until late in the evening. They had many questions about Savannah and Leo's time there. He and Maggie enter-tained the group with stories about kayaking and their beach adventures. Finally, they all went to their rooms or their nearby homes. When Leo walked Maggie to her room, they stalled in the doorway, not wanting to part from one another.

"Thank you for bringing me to Italy," she said shyly. "And thank you for bringing me to your home. I love it here."

He placed his arm on the doorjamb above her and leaned in. "I love you being here, too," he said almost in a whisper and slowly closed the distance between their lips. He kissed her deeply as her arms wrapped around his waist, pulling him in closer. When they heard someone coming up the stairs behind them, Leo pulled back, shaking his head that they had been interrupted.

"I'll never look at this doorway the same," he said, teasing her. "Goodnight, Maggie. Sleep well."

"Goodnight, Leo," she said, still reeling from the intensity of his kiss. Shutting the door behind her, she fell into the bed and fell asleep with her clothes still on. She did sleep well, never waking even once.

21

SANT' ERASMUS

Maggie woke to unfamiliar sounds. It was still dark outside, so she lay still and listened. The clanging of pots and pans and the sound of gentle laughter were like music to her ears. The only word to describe the sound was "family." She was eager to be a part of it, so she threw on a pair of jeans and a T-shirt and made her way down the stairs. When they noticed Maggie, each person welcomed her with, "*Buongiorno,* Maggie." It was such a simple and everyday scene to them but one that Maggie would never forget: the family sitting happily with one another enjoying a meal together.

As soon as Leo's sister noticed Maggie standing idle, she asked if Maggie could please hold her toddler, little John, while she helped another child fix some juice. Maggie happily took the child and placed him on her hip. She was so thankful for her friendship with Kathleen and her many children. She carried John to look out the window as the sun made its appearance in the sky. Leo was quickly at her side. "*Buongiorno bella*," he said, and smiled at her playfully.

She returned the grin, noticing his unshaved morning stubble and how green it made his eyes appear. "Good morning to you. Sleep well?"

"Oh yes, I always do when I'm home. Now hand me over this crazy kid, and you go grab some breakfast before it's cleared. We have a busy day today," he said as he tickled little John under his chin. Maggie handed over the toddler and watched Leo in amazement, thinking how lucky he was to always have little ones around and what a great father he would be because of it. She might have watched him a little too long, thinking about the two of them with a baby. He made eye contact with her, smiled, and motioned her towards the food with his free hand.

Maggie fixed a plate, sat down, and watched the coming and going of the people in the room. New faces appeared at the door saying, "*Buongiorno!*" They helped themselves to coffee and breakfast as they had done hundreds of times before. As more and more people passed through, she realized these were the many hands that worked the family farm. She glanced at the clock reading 7:00 and quickly did the math, figuring it was 1:00 a.m on Tybee Island – a world away.

After each person made their way into the various fields with full bellies, Leo showed Maggie around Sant' Erasmus. They set out in a truck of sorts that Leo called the "A Pay," but when Maggie looked at the back of the vehicle, it was written "Ape." It had a tiny cab, and a large bed on the back used to transport vegetables. Leo laughed as she walked wearily around the mini truck wondering how two adults could sit in the small cab.

"I promise, you'll be fine. It's been hauling us around for years. We will just be sitting very close inside." He lifted his eyebrows up and down, teasing her, and she swatted him on the arm. "I volunteered to be the delivery boy today while I show you around," he said. "Mario was happy to get the day off."

They settled in the cab that resembled a clown car from the circus. The cramped quarters pushed her up next to Leo. Every time he turned the wheel, even a bit, his hand would rub against her leg, and his elbow would brush her arm. His touch was electric, and she became grateful for the intimate seating.

Their first stop was the only hotel on the island, Il Lato Azzurro. The gateway read *"Ristorante,"* and they followed it to the back of the large house converted into a hotel. As Leo unloaded the produce, Maggie walked to the front of the house and up its large staircase. It reminded her of the older homes on Tybee that had porches built to accommodate the breezes in the heat of the summer. She sat at one of the small bistro tables that looked over the ocean. Once again, she felt the familiarity of life on an island.

Her silence was interrupted by a persistent little beep that she assumed to be someone's alarm clock in the hotel but laughed when she realized it was the horn on the Ape. Leo tried to get her attention and motioned for her to join him. As they crammed back into the truck, she turned her shoulders toward the door to try to allow for more room. This time, his hand playfully smacked her derriere. He tried to contain his laughter, but was failing miserably.

"I hear you snickering, and I know why. You better watch it, buddy," she told Leo, as his chuckle turned into a full-blown laugh.

They traveled to a supermarket and unloaded many different items: potatoes, carrots, tomatoes, and melons. The next stop was just around the corner, the church of Cristo Rey. As they pulled up, Maggie noticed a woman sprinkling something around the perimeter of the church. She wore a long black coat with a hood that resembled a cape. Maggie was fascinated by the bright orange curl peeking from beneath the hood and stared hard, trying to get a better look at the woman's face. As if on cue, the woman looked up, and their eyes locked. Leo waved to her casually as they passed, but something about the woman had stuck with her. Maggie then focused past her, "This is your parish church you told us about at the retreat. You described it so well."

"Yes, we supply fruit and vegetables for the rectory. Let me show you the church, and then we can take the produce over."

The church was small, with a center aisle and short pews comparable to her parish on Tybee Island. It had a Spanish feel with a dark wood ceiling and many arches. She walked around the perimeter. On her way out, she noticed the gruesome painting of *The Martyrdom of Saint Erasmus* which was in honor of the island's namesake. She stopped and stared as Leo joined her. "When I was a boy, I was scared to death of this picture. I wondered what bad things this man did to be tortured like this, so I was always an angel in church."

"Not always!" said a voice from behind, causing Maggie to jump. Leo started laughing as he turned to greet the voice.

The very young and handsome priest stood grinning, wearing a long cassock and a black beret of sorts. He and Leo embraced like brothers, patting each other on the back. As they separated, the priest said, "So very happy to see you home, my friend."

He extended his hand, "You must be Maggie. I've heard a lot about you." She sheepishly looked over at Leo, then took his hand. He pulled her towards him and gave her a traditional Italian welcome, kissing both her cheeks. "Welcome to Sant' Erasmus, and to Cristo Rey. I'm Giovanni Medici, but you can call me 'Father G.' I was always the one trying to get Leo in trouble in church when he was a lad. Now I'm the one trying to get him out of trouble with the big guy," he said as he pointed upward. Maggie liked him immediately.

He draped an arm around each of their shoulders and walked them towards the church entrance. They each grabbed a crate of produce and followed the path around to the rectory. As they opened the kitchen door, Maggie smelled bread and got caught sniffing the air. "Come, have a seat. It just came out of the oven," Father G said.

As she made her way to the table, she noticed a half-cracked door directly off the kitchen. Maggie peeked in and saw a red-haired lady kneeling beside an older priest sitting in a chair. She held a teacup in her hand and slowly helped him drink. It was the same woman who had been on the outskirts of the church earlier. The woman caught Maggie staring and quickly got to her feet to shut the door, leaving Maggie feeling guilty for intruding.

"I would love some of your bread, but I certainly don't want to interrupt anything."

"Nonsense," the young priest said as he sliced her off a chunk of the glazed loaf that had a thin slice of candied blood orange on top. She took a bite; her eyes widened with pleasure. The glaze was blood orange also and had hardened on the sweet vanilla cake. The combination was delicious.

The priest let out a hardy laugh, "Your reaction shows your approval. Thank you."

After a short visit in which Leo and Father G caught up on the past few months, Father G placed his beret back onto his curly brown hair, and they walked out the door back to the truck. He gave Maggie two pieces of cake he had wrapped in foil and pushed off on his bike with the long black cassock flapping in the wind.

"He's quite a character, isn't he?" Maggie asked.

"You have no idea!"

"Who was the older priest?"

"That was Father Misto. He was the pastor at Cristo Rey for many years until he became ill. That's when they brought in Father G to help. But lately, he has been doing much more than helping. Father Misto's health has been declining quickly. God bless him."

They wedged back into the Ape and drove toward their last stop. After traveling by Torre Massimiliano, a circular-shaped fort sitting at the end of the island, they stopped at a restaurant, Al Bacan. The restaurant had a lovely terrace with lots of small umbrellaed tables that overlooked the beach area, and the menu looked amazing. Al Bacan's owner excitedly dug into the boxes and planned their daily menu accordingly. Several patrons began to stroll in as it drew closer to lunchtime. Maggie thought of the restaurants at home, knowing the locals led the way to the best restaurant food. She smiled, thinking what a large part Leo's family played in this.

22

LIFE ON THE CANAL

Leo and Maggie walked inside and were greeted by the warmth and aroma of the large welcoming kitchen. Leo groaned as he realized everyone had finished lunch and made their way back into the fields. He walked straight to the stove and lifted the lid on a giant pot. His mother appeared out of nowhere and popped his hand with a long-neck wooden spoon. The clang of the lid's quick-release rang through the air as she said, "You're late, Leo. The food has been put away," with a teasing smile on her face.

"Oh pleeeease, Mama. It smells so good. Can't I still fix a plate?" he begged.

"There is none left for you," his mama said as she glanced at Maggie and winked. She then added, "Maggie, come fix you some lunch."

Maggie smiled and obeyed, wondering how many times he had been late for a meal in the past. Leo followed behind Maggie, but after Mrs. Vianello dished Maggie's plate, she shut the lid on Leo, making him groan even louder. It was funny to see a grown man revert to being a child with his mama.

"Come on, Mama. I'm a growing boy," Leo pleaded.

"Only if you help me with something. The two large planters on the porch need to be brought under the tarp; there's a cold front coming through tonight. Go and move them for your old mama, and I'll think about letting you fix a plate." Leo stalked off dutifully like an obedient middle schooler while Maggie stood frozen in the middle of the kitchen, not knowing what to do next.

"Come, eat, Maggie. Sit with me in the kitchen while I clean up from lunch." Maggie sat, and Mrs. Vianello continued, "It always amazes me what a man will do for food. My daughters would say, 'Forget it, I'll fix my own plate.' But a man thinks he will die if there is food available and not offered to them." Maggie giggled in conspiracy with Mrs. Vianello, but then she caught Maggie completely off guard. "Now, tell me how you feel about my Leo?" Thankfully Maggie was saved when Leo returned from outside, eager for his meal. His mama patted Maggie's hand, "We will finish this discussion later."

While they washed their plates off from lunch and placed them on the drying rack, Leo suggested Maggie take a nap. "You yawned all through lunch, and I wanted to show you Venice this afternoon around 4:00. I want to take you to one of my favorite dinner spots."

As she lay in bed, trying to fall asleep, she thought about being at the retreat on Tybee and how Leo had explained Venice and Carnivale. She finally dozed off with visions of masks and feathers and woke up with flutters in her stomach, excited to see Venice. The temperature dropped again that afternoon. As they walked out the door, Maggie pulled on the warm, wool coat she'd borrowed from Agnes, who had lived near Chicago. She laughed when she found a receipt in the pocket for five bar drinks with no food.

Leo took the scenic route into Venice so Maggie could see the city's splendor from the water. They traveled straight toward the tower of Saint Mark's Cathedral, then down through the middle of the Grand Canal. Magnificent houses and buildings sat directly on the water, some of their first floors completely submerged. Maggie had seen so many pictures of Venice, but to see it first hand was eerily beautiful.

Turning off the Grand Canal, they traveled down a small and quiet canal. The buildings surrounding it created a welcoming neighborhood, with laundry hanging out on a clothesline, and the gentle sounds of conversations and children playing filled the air. Leo had pulled the throttle back until they were almost idle, and the water carried them along slowly. They came to a stop beside a dark building where he tied the boat off to two pilings peeping out of the water.

"Where are we?"

"We are on the Rio Della Sensa." He pointed towards a dark house, "This once was my father's home, and now it belongs to me."

She studied the sturdy grey two-story building which had a weathered blue door facing the canal. There were three windows to the right of the door, but on the left was an open courtyard with a large arched doorway enclosed by an iron gate. Leo held out his hand to help her out of the boat.

Once inside the house, she was overwhelmed by the smell of saltwater and mud. It was a smell she knew all too well. It instantly reminded her of the inside of the Cockspur Lighthouse where she and Leo had kayaked.

A small entry led to a stairway straight ahead. They climbed the stairs that opened into a white plastered room with dark hardwood floors. The furniture scattered around the room was covered with sheets. Maggie walked around quietly, studying her surroundings – a one-room loft with a small kitchenette and bathroom, a door that led out to the back of the house, and a door that led onto a balcony overlooking the canal. The room had windows that overlooked the courtyard. "Your father grew up here?"

"Yes, although it was the whole house at that time. After my nonno died fifteen years ago, my father partitioned this side of the house and added another entrance to rent the rest of the house. The rental is enough to pay for the whole thing. I sometimes come here and sleep on the couch if I can't make it back to Sant' Erasmus, but as you can see, it has no electricity or water, so I don't come often."

She followed Leo down the stairs and out the door. The courtyard held a blue and white tiled fountain that no longer sprayed water, a wrought iron table and chairs, and many planters scattered around. A small tree, whose will to live outweighed its probability, had popped up in the back corner, "Oh Leo, I love it out here!" she exclaimed as she continued to walk around the garden. The canal could be seen through the large iron gated archway. It was a space that once held happiness and memories, and the fact that it was empty saddened Maggie. "Do you ever want to live here?"

"Not right now. My home is Sant'Erasmus."

"You could rent both sides out."

"I could, but I've got another idea. Can we talk about it over dinner?"

When they exited the building, Leo walked to a gondola that was moored alongside the courtyard. A flutter of excitement ran through Maggie as he helped her into the seat. She watched as he expertly untied the boat, pushed off the dock with his foot, and began to maneuver down the canal with skill. She was spellbound. She now understood how every woman who takes a gondolier ride while in Venice falls a little bit in love with their gondolier. He caught her stare and rewarded her with a broad smile.

The biting nip of the evening air announced the approaching dusk, but she barely felt it; she was spellbound by the beauty of Venice. Once they arrived at the restaurant, an inviting atmosphere welcomed them as they walked inside. They settled into a table by the window, looking over the darkening canal. Everyone seemed to know Leo and greeted him in Italian. He answered them affectionately, like family. "When working as a gondolier, I would eat here several times a week. My family supplies their produce, and all of their dishes are fresh. Would you like me to order some wine?"

"I'd love for you to order everything. I'm just going to sit back and enjoy." She had never done that before and couldn't believe she trusted someone enough to give him control of her choices. The simplicity of the act showed her how much she trusted Leo and excited her for their possible future.

As if reading her mind, he uttered in a low and sexy

voice, "You must trust me. I'm honored," and reached across the table and held her hand.

Her face was on fire. What was wrong with her? She knew that her heart was drawn to Leo, but she felt like a schoolgirl with a major crush after watching him in the gondola. She was in awe. He was oblivious to how he was affecting her as he rubbed his thumb across the top of her hand. Thankfully, the waiter saved her by bringing a bottle of Leo's choice of merlot to the table and pouring them a generous glass.

Maggie had almost regained control of her feelings when the food began to be served. They feasted on appetizers of artichoke chips with bean dip and sauteed scallops, an order of deep-fried fish, and a serving of pasta in a savory meat sauce. Leo bragged that the plate of seasonal vegetables had come straight from his family's farm.

As the meal came to an end, the waiter brought them a small glass of limoncello. Maggie took small sips, savoring its lemony burn as it glided down her throat and feeling the heat rise to her face. Leo noticed her smiling face was flushed from the liqueur. "You look relaxed and pleased," he paused and held her stare, "and also very beautiful."

Maggie glanced down at the table, then back into his eyes. "Is that the wine talking, or you?"

"Maybe a bit of both. I'm able to say that because of the wine, but it's something I've been trying to tell you for weeks now. You're beautiful, inside and out. I don't know how you agreed to come to Italy with me. I'm honored and feel like a lucky man."

"Thank you, Leo. I feel lucky, too, to be here with you." She took a sip of her wine, then intentionally changed the subject before she blurted out how sexy she thought he was. "So, tell me about your idea for your father's place."

Her question broke the romantic mood as he sat up and excitedly started talking. "Remember when I asked you to come to Venice with me and how I told you I wanted to try a kayak business? We could run it out of my father's place. We could store the kayaks in the courtyard, fix them up, and get the fountain running again. The loft could be the office, and we could run groups down the canal, staying away from the real touristy places and showing people a part of Venice that few see from the water. We could take them inside of the churches and buildings that are partly underwater and hike on many of the barrier islands." He spoke so fast she could hardly process what he was saying. The wine had loosened his tongue, and sometimes he switched to Italian until Maggie checked him back to English. "What do you think?"

Maggie said only one word, "We?"

A look of confusion passed over Leo's face. "Remember that day at your house when I asked you if you could come to Venice and help me? That's why I say 'we.' What's the matter? You look upset. Is it a bad idea?"

Maggie realized that if Leo started this business, and it was a success, he would forever live in Venice. She had no intention of leaving Savannah, so where would that leave them? She didn't want another relationship to come to an end with her being alone again. She wasn't sure her heart could take it. She carefully chose her words, "Is this what you truly want?"

Again, he looked puzzled, ignorant of the pain in her heart. "Have you been listening to me? It could be wonderful, no? I could quit being a gondolier completely and do something that I love. You showed me that."

"Then I'll help you. But you must remember that I go home in less than fourteen weeks. That's non-negotiable." Then she added, "No matter what."

Leo nodded his head yes but missed the hurt in Maggie's voice. He was on cloud nine and immediately started making plans. As he told her about Murano and the hiking trails they could include on a trip, he realized she was half-listening. He thought she was jet-lagged from the trip, so he paid the bill and escorted her to the boat.

The ride back to Sant' Erasmus was very different from the boat ride over. Her hurt boiled into a fit of deep anger in the pit of her stomach. *How was I so love-struck just an hour ago?* She wondered. She knew the answer; it was always a man behind the wheel of a boat, or in this case, behind the fórcula. The more she thought about helping him, the angrier she became. *He is just using me to help him start a business and hopes to romance me in the process and then send me on my merry way.* When he reached over to hold her hand, she slid it away and fiddled with her wind-blown hair. As the boat slowed once they came closer to Sant' Erasmus, Leo tried to pull her closer, but she moved towards the front.

She watched the buoys and the lights as they came into the canal, but then she noticed something moving in a small field. As they got closer, she could make out the shape of a woman holding a small lantern. She wore a long coat with a cape-like hood. Maggie recognized it immediately. It was the woman from the church. *What in the world is she doing walking in a field alone at midnight?* Maggie wondered and shivered as a chill ran up her spine. She watched the figure as they passed and continued watching until all she could see was a dot from the light of the lantern.

Once Leo docked at the farm, he offered her his hand to help her out. She refused it and swiftly walked towards the house while he secured the boat. He caught up with her quickly and gently grabbed her arm. "I had a wonderful time with you tonight," he said in a whisper as he leaned in for a kiss. She turned her head so that it landed on her cheek. Saying goodnight, she walked straight up to her bedroom, cursing herself for opening her heart.

The next morning, Maggie got up and went to breakfast with the family. She intentionally avoided Leo, and when everyone stood to leave, Maggie left with them. Leo's mom watched her walk out, then angrily swatted Leo on his shoulder, "What did you do?"

"Ow! I don't know, Mama. One minute we were fine; in fact, we were better than fine, then the next minute she was angry with me."

"Well, you'd better figure out why. I like that girl."

Leo grabbed his jacket and raced out the door, stumbling to catch up with Maggie. "Hey, where are you heading?"

She didn't look up but replied, "I'm going on a walk."

"Want some company?"

"No thanks," she said aloud and prayed he would just turn around and leave her alone for a while. She kept walking down the path, and when she looked back, he was no longer following.

Leo was confused by Maggie. He couldn't read what was going through her mind. Shaking his head, he jumped on a bike sitting beside the house and rode in the opposite direction to the rectory. Father G had just finished daily Mass and was sitting at his kitchen table having his first cup of coffee. "Good morning, Leo. Where's Maggie?"

Leo shrugged, "She's on a walk, and she wanted to be alone."

"What did you do?"

"Why does everyone keep asking me that? Nothing. I did nothing."

"Backtrack and explain."

Leo began with them leaving on their date and told his friend everything, ending with the events that morning. His friend swatted him, just like his mom had, but at least he offered some possible explanations. "You've told me before that you never dated much because you hadn't met many women you wanted to date. But tell me, how do you feel about Maggie?"

"If I'm being honest, I really like her. I could actually see myself being married to her and having a family." He shook his head in disbelief, "Wow, I just said that out loud."

"Yeah, you did, my friend. Now, tell me, where do you see that happening?"

"I haven't really thought about it."

"Well, believe me, Maggie has. She knows that if you have a successful business in Venice, you will never settle down in the States with her. Now, she has to decide if she's going to help you with your business or if she is going to fall in love with you. She can't do both."

Leo plopped in the chair beside his friend. "How did I not catch that? She asked me if the business was what I really wanted. I didn't know it was a choice. What should I do?"

"Talk to her. Only together can you come up with a solution." Leo hugged Father G, ran out the door, and eagerly retraced Maggie's path. He wasn't surprised where he found her.

~

MAGGIE WALKED to where she always found comfort, the beach. She sat on the cold sand and said her morning prayer.

Good morning, God
Today I give you all my work and all my play
All I do, and all I say.
I love you, God. Amen

Rolling her eyes, Maggie smiled, wondering why she still prayed the same morning offering as when she was a little girl. Perhaps its very simplicity continued its relevance. She concentrated on the word "all" and the weight that it held. If she genuinely was giving everything to God, she knew in her heart that she had to help Leo. There was a chance she would lose him in the long run. But he deserved to be happy, even if that meant he would be in Venice and she would be in Savannah. Once she decided she would help Leo, a huge weight lifted from her heart.

She stayed a while longer, enjoying the sounds of the seagulls and waves. Eventually, the chill of the sand made its way through the jeans she was wearing. When she began to get up, Leo plopped down beside her.

He ran his hand down her arm and laced his fingers into hers. He quickly began to talk, afraid she might sprint off again. "There is a very good chance that I'm falling for you." That got her attention, and she listened intently. "I know that's very confusing, with us trying to start this business and you going back to the States in three months, but I know if we work together, we can figure it all out. I think we are worth it, don't you?"

Maggie bit her lip and started nodding but quickly began shaking her head. "How? How in the world could this ever work? I want this for you, I really do. You deserve to be happy, and I truly think this business will succeed. But I'm not sure where that will leave us."

"Are you willing to try, Maggie? Just say yes. Say yes, and I promise that we *can* figure this out together."

An apprehensive smile grew until it spread across her face, "*Yes*! Let's figure this out."

Leo lifted her chin and kissed her softly on the lips. Smiling, he took her hand. "Are you ready to go?"

"Yes, I'm freezing out here." But when they walked toward the bicycle, she shook her head no. Leo motioned to the handlebars, and she said, "Oh no! I haven't ridden on handlebars since Mike Bryson gave me a ride home from the beach in ninth grade when I lost my flip flops on Tybee and the pavement was burning my feet." She pulled up the arm on her jacket and pointed to the large scar on her forearm. "That's what happened to me, twenty-two stitches."

"You told me last night you trusted me."

"Yes, but that was picking out my meal at the restaurant, not balancing me on two wheels."

He lowered his head and extended his hand. "I've got you. Don't you trust me?"

She eyed him warily, "Yes." Then she narrowed her gaze and added, "But don't let me down."

He nodded once, realizing she was referring to much more than a bike ride. "Hop on!" Leo gently leaned her back and cradled her against his chest, unlike young Mike. She was amazed at how much she trusted him about many things, and she treasured their ride home.

23

DAVIDE

While Leo chased Maggie around all day, a delivery arrived at the farm's dock. Davide signed the delivery ticket for the large packages. He was surprised to find two kayaks when he'd removed the black plastic covering. Davide dug through the trash and realized they had been addressed to Leo. "My bad," he mumbled to himself.

He studied the boats and ran his hand around the cockpit. He vaguely remembered overhearing a conversation between Leo and his dad. His father had just returned from Savannah and explained to Leo that his childhood friend, Maggie, owned a kayaking company. Davide wondered, *What are those two up to?*

Later that evening, Davide was finally able to tell Leo about the delivery. Davide noticed the excitement spread across Leo's face and followed him when he dashed off to find Maggie and excitedly pulled her down to the dock.

"Something was delivered today. Come on, slowpoke," Leo teased.

"No way!" she yelled when she saw her two kayaks from home. But as she got closer, she noticed that these were new and was impressed that Leo had matched the ones from Tybee. "Leo, I love them! They are exactly like mine."

Davide trailed behind them, watching and listening, until he got up the nerve to approach them. "So, are you starting a kayak company in Venice?"

His voice had startled the two of them, and they quickly looked up, but the smiles that crossed their faces showed Davide he had guessed correctly. "That's what we are hoping for," Leo answered.

"Are you hiring?"

Leo gave a questioning look at his brother, "What do you mean, Davide? You love the farm."

Davide nodded, "I love the farm because it is our home, but the time has long come for me to leave. The girls and their husbands have been running this place. Maybe it's time for their little brother to make his own way. With Anna working such late shifts at the hospital in the city, we rarely see each other. It would be good to be closer."

Leo could understand his brother wanting to leave the farm. Their older sisters had married men who were indispensable on the farm; each of them had families with strong sons who were now working the farm full-time. The farm was running quite well. Davide was very comfortable on the water. Although he had never been on a kayak, Leo had no doubt he could be taught easily. And to top it off, his girlfriend lived in Venice, so he would love an excuse to work near her.

Maggie nudged Leo, "I've seen that same look in someone else's eyes when they were asking me for a job, and that person turned out to be the Savannah Gondolier."

Leo hugged his brother, "I pray we get this up and running, and if we do, I would be honored to have you onboard." Knowing that they now had a future employee made Leo more determined than ever.

Leo and Maggie spent the next several days on the waterways around Venice. It was cold, but they wore long johns underneath their clothes and covered them with fleece jackets. Leo took her to many unique spots that only a kayak could reach. Some places were serene and made peaceful by the water, but some locations were eerie, as if the water came in one day and just covered up people's daily lives. The churches were the prettiest, withstanding the water with grace. Their tall arched windows let in plenty of light that illuminated the interior. Leo was correct when he explained that the people in kayaks could see things others couldn't. Maggie felt confident he could have a very successful business.

They also explored the many camping areas on the various islands close enough to their shove-off point and calculated the tides and timetables for getting there. Next, they began cleaning Leo's loft area and courtyard. He had the electricity and water re-connected and even had the fountain in the courtyard flowing once again. After two weeks, they wrote a reasonable business plan and had an appointment to present it to the city for approval. Although it had been delayed until January because of the Christmas holidays, they continued to make progress on the schedule they had set.

Proud of their hard work, Leo suggested they take a night off and took Maggie back to his favorite little restaurant right down the canal. This time, they were seated at a cozy table in the corner of the room. Leo offered to take the seat against the wall to give her the best view. Once they were settled, they were casually greeted by the owner and staff while water was brought to their table.

Leo smiled at Maggie, but his eyes drifted from her face to over her shoulder, and the smile quickly left his mouth. Maggie followed his eyes to see a young man who forcefully threw both his napkin and money on the table as he stood and turned. He exited the restaurant leaving the door hanging open. Before he walked off, she noticed he pulled his coat over the black and white striped shirt worn by gondoliers.

"Have a great night, Michael," the waitress shouted behind him and shook her head as she collected the money scattered on the table.

"Who was that?" Maggie asked.

"A fellow gondolier. Actually, not just any gondolier; he's family. Although it's never really felt like that. He was also the man who witnessed my father's death and the same man who told the police it was all my dad's fault."

"I'm so sorry, Leo. Let's just leave."

"No!" he answered, a little too intensely. Then he shook his head and ran his fingers through his hair. "Tonight, we celebrate." A smile slowly came back to his face, but a worried crease remained between his eyes.

They enjoyed another fabulous meal of mini pork belly porchetta, Venetian style veal, and a plate of seasonal vegetables that had changed entirely in the two weeks since their last visit. They finished their meal with tiramisu and limoncello.

After walking out of the restaurant arm-in-arm, Leo asked if she would be interested in going back to the house at Rio Della Sensa for a nightcap. Maggie knew this nightcap could lead to unchartered waters, but her heart ached to be alone with him, so she said yes.

Leo lit a fire in the large brick fireplace, and they cuddled under a blanket in front. Everything felt perfect. They had nowhere to be, and no one was listening from the next room. They focused only on each other. Slowly running his hand along the side of her face and down her neck, he asked with his eyes if he could continue. She nodded with approval. Their kisses deepened as they slowly explored every inch of each other until their passion swelled into slow lovemaking. At long last, they fell asleep holding each other tightly and praying the morning would hold out as long as possible.

24

THE TOURIST

Leo worked on the farm that Saturday. They were enclosing the greenhouse crops which had stood open all summer and fall. Maggie had volunteered to help, but they needed big strong men to lift the heavy plastic sheets. She took the opportunity to visit Venice on her own.

Maggie left the house early so she wouldn't miss the 7:45 a.m. boat to Venice, but underestimated the biting cold wind coming off the water. She focused on the Vaporetto dock as she made her way against the loud gusts of wind. She didn't notice when a bicycle flew out from a nearby driveway. Had she been two steps closer, she would have been knocked on her rump.

She recognized the dark jacket and the cape-like hood as the woman waved her hand and yelled out, *"Scusi!"* But the woman never even glanced back. The bicycle's front basket was piled high with packages. Plants hung over its edges and were knocked around by the wheels' spin. Maggie wondered where she was going in such a hurry early in the morning. Maggie looked at the driveway where the dust was still circulating from the woman's speedy departure. Beside the mailbox sat a blue painted sign that read, "Flowers & Herbs." Intrigued, she knew she would stop in for a visit on another day.

By the time she made it to the dock, Maggie was shivering. She waited for the many people to climb off, both workers and tourists alike, but she was the only one getting on. She welcomed the warmth that enveloped her as she stepped through the open vaporetto doors.

The ride took longer than she expected, making two stops on the way. She decided to relax, enjoy the scenery and read the romance novel she had tucked away in her traveling backpack. But as Venice started coming into view, she quickly stowed it away and sat back to enjoy the scenery. She was excited that she could take her time and meander around the city on her own.

She disembarked at the Fondameta Nuove stop. She knew enough about the city's layout to reason that if she walked in the opposite direction from the water, without crossing the Grand Canal, she would eventually run into Saint Mark's Cathedral. However, once she began to walk through the turns and twists of the ancient walkways, she lost her bearings and no longer knew which way she was going.

After going over a small bridge marked "Ponte Della Tette" she decided to ask for help. She noticed several people walking toward a setback brick building with tables and stands out front filled with postcards and paintings, but mainly with books. The handmade sign at the end of the table was written in Italian, but had a smaller English translation underneath. "Welcome to the most beautiful bookstore in the world." The sign drew her in; she made her way towards the entrance and glanced up at the hanging fabric sign that read "Libreria Acqua Alta."

Maggie loved bookstores; a tingle of excitement ran through her as she entered. Once inside, she stopped and glanced around as a slow smile spread across her face. She'd never experienced a bookstore that made such an artistic statement; this was a place like no other. There were books and paraphernalia everywhere and cats lounging upon every flat surface. Most of the books were stacked randomly on tables and shelves, intermingled with pictures, figurines, masks, and toys. But the most interesting things were the full-size boats, gondolas, and bathtubs placed between the many paths. Some were sitting on the floor, and some were placed on their sides. It was like walking through a garden that held books instead of flowers.

She walked down the aisles, picked up various items she wanted to purchase, and then came to a door leading to a small outdoor courtyard. Once outside, she gasped when she saw the stairway on the back wall built entirely with books. How had it withstood rain, snow, and floods? But there it stood, completely sturdy. People were able to climb the stairway of stories to a small platform at the top that looked over the canal. She knew she had to give it a try.

She warily climbed each step, some of them slightly absorbing her weight into the paper the books were printed on, but the view was worth it. Part of the beauty was the incredible journey to the top. Like Venice itself, these old books had been traveled over by many and still remained beautiful.

After covering every inch of the entire store, she found a robust man sitting beside a gold metal cash register with three cats draped on the table around him. As he finished ringing up her order, she asked for directions. "I'm trying to find my way to St. Mark's. I came over the Delle Telle and am lost."

Two young girls behind her in line started giggling, which made the man break into a hearty laugh. Maggie didn't know what she had said and began to blush as she looked from the girls to him questioningly. The man hushed the girls behind her and explained in his very broken English. "Many years ago, this sezione was used for...how you say? Prostituzione? 'Ponte Della Tette' means," he cleared his throat and gestured towards his massive chest, "'Boob Bridge.' You say you came over the Boob. It made us laugh. *Mi dispiace.* I no mean to offend."

Maggie joined in laughing and apologized for her mistake that he waved off. Then she asked, "While I'm asking dumb questions, what does *'acqua alta'* mean?"

"*Acqua alta è il floods.* They come when the lagoon rises. The boats, the bathtubs, and tabelle protect the books. The staircase, I non salvage."

Maggie nodded with respect for the lost books while picturing all the people working to salvage the mess. It reminded her of when she would return to Tybee after a hurricane and spend weeks cleaning up the damage. Nature's fury could be devastating. "Thank you for sharing this lovely bookstore with the world," she said with a smile.

He grinned with pride, then handed her a tourist map and drew a path in red marker to Saint Mark's.

She left the shop thinking how small businesses had so much personality. A shop was a way for the owner to share with the world what they love. It should bring happiness both to the owner and all who shop in it. She felt blessed to have experienced it firsthand.

Maggie followed the red lines on the map, which ran along many tiny passageways until, much to her astonishment, it opened right into the piazza at Saint Mark's. She walked straight to the long entrance line for the basilica and entered behind a private tour guide escorting an older English couple. She stayed close to them, eavesdropping on information about Saint Mark himself and putting the church into a historical context with the world around it at that time.

Looking at churches built in the ninth century made Maggie realize how young America was. Eventually, the guide began to take notice of Maggie, so she moved ahead of the threesome; nonetheless, they were directly behind her as she descended into the crypt. Again, she moved slowly to listen and show her respect to the evangelist, Mark.

Exiting the basilica, she walked towards the center of the piazza to admire the colossal Byzantine basilica, Doge's Palace, and the tall brick bell tower of the campanile. The buildings flanked the only piazza in the city. As she turned slowly to take in her surroundings, she realized the tour guide from Saint Marks had walked up behind her, and Maggie spun right into her. Maggie nervously looked up, waiting to be reprimanded.

"I know you," the guide said.

"I don't think so."

"I do. You're Leo's girlfriend, the American. I've seen the two of you in boats along Della Sensa."

Surprised, Maggie thrust out her hand. "I'm Maggie. I'm very sorry I intruded on your tour of St. Marks, but you were so interesting I couldn't stop myself from listening to you." The guide shook Maggie's hand, but said nothing as she gave Maggie a once over, sizing her up. Maggie continued, "I only have a few hours in Venice today and would love to see more sights. Could you show me around? I can pay you. I'll even buy your lunch."

The guide slowly smiled. "I'd love to. My name's Katerina. But I must warn you, I eat like two men combined."

"Deal!" Maggie answered, liking Katerina immediately and happily putting away the city's tourist map.

25

MOST ELIGIBLE BACHELOR

Maggie followed Katerina down a few side streets away from San Mark's and quickly came to a section, Le Mercerie, known for its world-class shopping. Maggie noticed the women were highly fashionable and wore short dresses, snug pantsuits, and high stilettos, even in the brisk weather. Although they were beautiful, Maggie was thankful for her walking boots and thick wool coat.

Once they hit the Grand Canal, they walked along its bordering path, filled with many bistros. As Maggie and Katerina came to the various street vendors, Katerina negotiated the price of two small, framed prints and a scarf. They walked upon the white-columned Rialto Bridge, the oldest bridge in Venice, and then traveled to the opposite side of the canal and through the Rialto market. They crossed the Grand Canal the next time on the Ponte Degli Scalzi; it was a totally different experience. As Maggie climbed the steps, she thought about the old Led Zeppelin hit "Stairway to

Heaven." The stairs appeared to go straight up to the sky. Looking forward made her head spin so she made her way over to the side to steady herself with the rail.

Katerina seemed almost giddy once they were on the other side of the bridge. "This is my neighborhood, Cannaregio." She stopped in front of a large church. "This is my parish church, the prettiest church in Venice, Chiesa degli Scalzi, which means the 'barefoot Carmelites.'"

Many of the churches in Europe felt like museums, but Maggie felt vibrant and reverent when she walked in this one. The church was massive with dark stained wood. They walked towards the front, genuflected, and went into a pew. Candles burned, signifying the active presence of Jesus in the tabernacle. After a brief silent prayer, they walked around the church quietly as Katerina shared its history.

As they were exiting the church, Maggie stopped Katerina and pointed to three poster prints near the exit. "We'll talk outside," Katerina mouthed, and after Maggie looked at the posters for a while longer, she followed. Katerina explained the posters of Our Lady of Loreto in great detail. Maggie couldn't wait to ask Leo about them the next time they had a chance to talk.

Making their way down another side street, Katerina pointed to her flat. They finished their tour with a very late lunch at a little wine bar off the beaten path. They both ordered a merlot, and true to her word, Katerina ordered enough for two large men. Maggie enjoyed cicchetti followed by pasta and finished with strawberry cheesecake. By the end of the meal, a slightly tipsy Katerina blurted out, "You do know that you landed one of the most eligible bachelors in Venice, don't you? Every girl in town has vied for that man's affection, present company included, and he never showed any interest in anyone."

Maggie was shocked by the way Katerina had unthinkingly spilled out her statement. She felt like an outsider which immediately made her defensive. "I didn't *land* anyone. Leo and I are friends." Katerina gave her a sideways look in disbelief, and Maggie corrected herself. Shaking her head, she admitted, "Leo and I were just friends, but I think it has evolved to something more." She smiled, "In fact, I'm pretty sure I've fallen for him."

Katerina laughed, "Well, of course you have. Get in line with hundreds of other women. The one difference is apparent; he's fallen for you, too." She refilled both of their glasses and took a long sip. "I didn't expect to like you. Not to be mean, but you see, Venetians talk, and the word on the street is that you were a snotty business owner from the States offering Leo a big job to move him away. I see now just how wrong that rumor is. You truly care for him, don't you?"

Maggie nodded her head and let out a long huff, "Yes. I didn't plan to, but I do."

"Well, welcome to Venice," and she wrapped both of her hands around Maggie's.

On the vaporetto back to Sant' Erasmus, Maggie thought about her conversation with Katerina. Doubt quickly wiggled its way back into her heart. How would this ever work? Katerina had said, "Welcome to Venice." Surely, she didn't think Maggie would be staying. And Leo, was he looking toward the future? He said they would work it out, but how was that possible?

Her brain was spinning, and she was warm both from the wine and the heater on the vaporetto. The rocking of the boat must have lulled her to sleep because the next thing she remembered was being shaken. She opened her eyes hazily to a burly Italian yelling at her, "You go. You go, lady!"

Darkness had enveloped the boat, and she was confused by her surroundings. "Huh? Where am I?"

"Sant' Erasmus. You go!"

Maggie stumbled towards the doorway, still half asleep and half tipsy, and grabbed the hand of someone who was helping her onto the dock. As she got to the top, she realized the hand belonged to Leo, and she broke out in an ear-to-ear grin. "Leo, I've missed you today."

He returned her smile, but seemed surprised, both by her statement and the smell of wine. "Oh, did you now?"

"Uh-huh."

"Well, I was worried about you. I got nervous when you didn't get off of the 5:05 vaporetto. I would have looked for you in Venice if you weren't on this one. Did you have a good day?"

"Oh yes. I made a friend."

"A friend? And does your friend have a name?" he asked, secretly hoping it wasn't a male's name.

"Her name is Katerina; she said she knew you."

Leo's insides rolled and retracted his previous thought; a male would have been much better than Katerina. Men were so much easier to deal with. "Yes, I know Katerina." He thought about Katerina coming to Sant' Erasmus and proclaiming her love. She had weaseled her way to their family dinner, then made him walk her to the same vaporetto dock he was now standing in front of. Then he remembered her screaming at him that he would never find anyone as wonderful as she was and stomping away down the dock. He was very anxious to hear what poison she had told Maggie. "How did you meet?"

Maggie was shivering, so Leo put his arm around her, pulling her close. They strolled down the path. Maggie told him about eavesdropping on Katerina's tour of St. Marks, the posters of the house of Loreto, and finally, she and Katerina sitting in the small wine bar. Maggie slowed to ensure that Leo was listening. "She told me she had come to Sant' Erasmus and threw herself on you. She said that you were kind and told her that she was a wonderful woman, bright and witty, but that your heart belonged to someone else. She said she had done her homework and knew you weren't seeing anyone, so she asked who. You told her that you hadn't met her yet, making her furious. Then you told her to follow her heart to the man God wished for her to be with. By that point in your conversation, she was so angry that she said horrible things. But, she told me that you were right." Leo stopped walking and bent down to listen more intently to Maggie. "She said that she didn't love you, not even a little and that she was just searching for a husband. She fell in love one year later and has now been married to the love of her life for five years."

Leo was shocked. He had seen Katerina a couple of times in passing but always ducked away to avoid an awkward conversation. He was delighted to hear the story's outcome and grateful to Katerina and Maggie for sharing. Maggie added, "She also said that she wasn't the first who had professed their love to you."

"Katerina is right about one of those things," he said with a gentle smile. He chose his next words slowly. "My heart did belong to someone else, and for the first time in my life, I know who that person is." He slowly turned Maggie towards him and looked down at her lips, then leaned in and kissed her gently. She melted into him as they stood on the dark path, opening themselves up to a future together, whatever and wherever that would be. Suddenly, she felt something wet on her face and pulled her head back from him to look up to the sky as the snow began to come down harder. He quickly kissed the end of her nose, took off his jacket to cover both of their heads, and they walked briskly back to the house.

26

PATTY

Maggie went for a bike ride the following morning and found herself at the end of the path that read "Flowers & Herbs," but this time, a smaller sign hung beneath that read "Open." Curious, she walked her bike inland along the curving road, following the smell of tea olives and winter jasmine and the sound of Jimmy Buffet happily playing. Realizing she had not heard American music since she had arrived, she happily began to strut toward the tune of "Margaritaville."

Like a true Parrot Head, she followed the music right onto the porch of a small white clapboard cottage where the melody was drifting through the opened top half of a Dutch door. Maggie looked around and felt the familiarity of the slow pace of beach living. The porch had a very Low Country feel, with a porch swing on one side flanked by two Adirondack chairs and a large metal sign that read "Patty's Plants—Come On In."

The porch held several potted plants of various sizes.

Most of the small pots had herbs that Maggie recognized, but she was startled by a group of larger plants. "Shit fire!" she cried out, looking from a distance. She slowly moved in to get a closer look. The exposed roots resembled a human baby and not in a cute and cuddly way. She had never seen anything like it and was so focused on the oddity of the plants she didn't hear the door open. She was surprised by the woman that stood in front of her.

"Don't be scared of me, dear."

Maggie gave the red-haired woman a once over, immediately recognizing her from the rectory. She was wearing overalls and her wild and curly hair was pulled back with a rolled-up bandana. She couldn't look less frightening if she tried. "Uh, why would I be scared of you?" Maggie asked but secretly thought about how the woman had appeared a few nights back along the shore.

A smile moved across her face, "You're American? How wonderful. Me, too. I saw you at Cristo Rey the other morning, but I didn't know you were from the States. My name's Patty."

"Hi Patty, I'm Maggie, and I'm actually living on the island for a few weeks. I love your home. But tell me about these plants; they are the oddest thing I've ever seen."

Patty eyed her guardedly. "These are my fake mandrake plants; they are actually Ficus ginseng that I manipulated to look this way. It's crazy how they look alive, isn't it?" She moved towards them, pinching off a dead leaf and smiling as she doctored it. "I don't have many local visitors. Welcome. Would you like a tour?" she asked as a small tabby cat gently rubbed against Maggie's leg. "Then maybe we can sit and warm ourselves in the sun. I know how much Cheeto would love that."

Maggie smiled at the name and reached down and rubbed behind the cat's ear. "I would love that," she said in response, wondering how her tabby, Joe, was doing and if he was keeping her yard safe and sound.

"You've already walked through some of the gardens. I grow fresh flowers, herbs, and seasonings. I ship a lot of seeds, herbs, and other items made from them to different parts of the world. That's what pays the bills. But I have a small local shop, too. Come on in."

They entered a large room with shiplap walls and floors of pine hardwood. One end of the room looked like an apothecary shop with many small glass jars of various herbs, creams, ointments, and bath salts. The far wall was lined with built-in bookshelves filled with different dried flowers that could be made into small bouquets or put into small cloth sachet bags for potpourri. There were window sill herb gardens, various scented candles, and a wide variety of soaps and shower gels. Scattered around were small coastal paintings, trivets, and all things nautical. Like a kid in a candy shop, Maggie wanted to touch everything.

After stopping at the wildflower bouquets, Maggie didn't realize she was smiling until Patty said, "I see how much you like the dried flowers; you're going to love my greenhouse." They walked out the back door; down a short, shelled path; and inside a greenhouse filled with blooming flowers of poppies, bells of Ireland, and many shades of delphiniums and larkspur. Maggie gasped, "Oh Patty, it's beautiful!"

"It is, isn't it?" Patty agreed and led Maggie around the covered garden. She explained how she used light control and carbon dioxide infusion for the indoor plants and used outdoor gardens for the warmer months. Right past the flowers were the herbs, and Patty called out the name of each one as she passed them, as if she was greeting them with a "hello". Chamomile, chives, eucalyptus, lemongrass, rosemary, sage, mint, lemon balm, lavender, garlic, and leeks. When they got to the back, Patty motioned to a sectioned-off area against a wall. "Back there are my unwanted guests, the genuine mandrakes." But then she quickly turned and walked back to the front.

She picked up a sharp locking blade knife from the potting bench and cut a blue delphinium in full bloom. Running it under water, she wrapped it in a small piece of wet cheesecloth, and handed it to Maggie. "This is for you. Are you staying on Sant' Erasmus alone?"

"Oh, heavens no. Quite the contrary. I'm staying with the Vianellos."

"They are a nice family. Well, some of them are anyway. Do you have time for a cup of tea?"

"I'd love that," Maggie said and took one last look at the colorful show of flowers. Her eyes focused on the mandrake section one last time, and she wondered why it was covered and separated from the other plants. Patty called to her, and they exited through the same door they had entered, but this time they followed a path to the back-side of the cottage. They entered a mudroom that opened into a cozy kitchen. It looked like it was straight out of *Southern Living* magazine. Maggie happily perched herself upon a barstool against the marble-top kitchen island. Patty put on the tea kettle, pulled a jar of fresh tea leaves, and placed them into two infusers. "I don't get many visitors from the island. Only the bee man, and I don't let him past my front porch."

"Why don't you get many local visitors?"

"You truly don't know, do you?" Maggie shook her head, no. "The islanders are scared of me. They call me 'Strega Straniera,' which means 'foreign witch.'"

"No way!" Maggie said quickly.

"Way!" Patty answered.

Maggie laughed as the conversation reminded her of being with the tribe. "Tell me everything," she said as she began to wander around Patty's kitchen. Maggie smiled at the many pictures of Patty and her husband and noticed the progression of his illness. There was a wedding picture, several travel pictures, and one of him sitting on the porch of her cottage wearing a large brim straw hat. A pair of rosary beads hung over the straw hat picture, causing Maggie to presume it was one of his last photos. His face held tired eyes, and his arms and legs were very thin. Maggie went back and picked up a beach picture of the couple and sat down at the kitchen island.

"My husband and I were drawn to Sant' Erasmus from the first time we stepped off the vaporetto. We were so happy together," she paused and looked at the picture that Maggie was holding of the two of them standing on a beach. She sighed and continued, "Early in our marriage, we learned we were unable to have children. As much as it saddened us, we leaned on each other, worked hard, and traveled often. We worked hard where we could also play hard. We were botanists and worked outside of Santa Barbara on the coast of California. On one of our many trips, we visited Sant'

Erasmus. It became our favorite place in the world, and we quickly realized why.

"Geographically, it's the same latitude as Lompoc Valley, so the vegetation felt just like home. So over time, we started buying land on the island, knowing that we would retire here. One of the pieces of land had a small cottage, so we started using all of our vacation time here, fixing it up and planting a few perennials, herbs, shrubs, and trees, things that didn't require maintenance, knowing we could really enjoy them one day.

"Shult Biotech approached us ten years ago, offering us a job researching plants to cure cancer. Knowing it was a once-in-a-lifetime chance, we jumped. The company's testing facilities would keep us living in the Santa Barbara area. However, we were not aware of what types of plants we would be researching. Come to find out, it was the mandrake.

"Mandrakes only grow in certain parts of the world with the same soil group, basic temperature, climate, and vegetation zone. That just happens to be in Southern California and in the Mediterranean. The plant itself has a mysterious background, to say the least. It has been used for over 4000 years. It was mentioned in the Bible as a drug for various healings, and also many pleasures." She paused and slightly wagged her eyebrows. "The mandrake can cure insomnia, tumors, ulcers, rheumatism, infertility, and convulsions. It was used as an anesthetic and said to expel demonic possession. Several people said it made them fly, but that has been proven incorrect. Since it is a hallucinogenic that makes people high, they only felt like they were flying. Over and

above all of that, it is highly poisonous and must be moni-
tored safely.

"My husband and I were very leery at first, but upon
further investigation found that the mandrake showed great
possibilities. They are made of the plant substance,
podophyllotoxin. Byproducts of this substance showed real
promise against many cancers by causing breaks in the DNA
strands by..." She looked at the blank look on Maggie's face
and laughed. "I'm so sorry for being a plant nerd. Long story
short, we were pretty sure we had come up with something
that could successfully be used in cancer treatment. That's
when it happened; we found out that Brett had cancer.

"Our research became unceasing until we finally realized
that time was not on our side. Even if we came up with the
perfect cure, we didn't have the time to run the trials and
then get it on the market. But we did have the right land to
grow the mandrake. We bought three plants and moved to
Sant' Erasmus to attempt to find a cure.

"Brett never left the lab and began working crazy hours,
usually all through the night. One morning I woke up and
found him lying on the ground with an empty cup in his
hand." Her voice cracked as she started to cry. She took a sip
of her tea and tried to continue. "He was trying something...well, to be honest, he was trying anything to ease his
pain and to find a cure." She grabbed a dishcloth from the
sink and wiped the tears that had been running steadily
down her face. "That was the last day that I stepped foot in
that lab. Five years ago this month."

Maggie stood and walked toward Patty to console her
and was surprised when Patty wrapped her in a tight hug.
While regaining her composure, she said, "I haven't divulged

my story to anyone in a long time. It actually was cathartic to share. Thank you."

"I'm honored you shared it with me," Maggie answered. "But I do have one small question. Why do the locals call you a witch?"

"Ah, that's a tricky one that I've tried to work out in my mind. I think the people on the island watched, what appeared to be, a very healthy Brett walk off the vaporeto when we moved here. Then he was being buried not so long afterward. He never left the house, so they didn't see the progression of his illness. The only one who really did was the bee man. Also, some saw me roaming the fields at night looking for evening primrose to ease his pain. I may have looked suspicious. But quite honestly, I haven't done anything to try and prove them wrong. I was sad and wanted to be left alone." She patted Maggie's hand, took a deep breath, and added, "But I think the time has now come to re-enter the world."

LEO HAD JUST FINISHED REPAIRING a window on the outside of the kitchen when Maggie arrived home. He helped her off the bike and immediately noticed she was holding a delphinium. As they walked into the kitchen, he asked, "Where did you get the flower from? Do you have a secret admirer?"

Mrs. Vianello was standing by the sink and took an immediate interest in their conversation. Maggie decided to see if the myth was true. "It was given to me by the *Strega Straniera*." As soon as it came out of her mouth, a glass plate slid from Mrs. Vianello's hands and hit the tiled floor. The sound pierced through the air. Maggie turned to see Mrs. Vianello staring directly at her with a look of cold fear on her face. "What did you say, child?"

Maggie looked over at Leo and then back to Mrs. Vianello. "Patty gave me the flower. I went to her shop today."

"And who is Patty?" she asked.

"Patty owns the flower shop across the street from the beach."

Mrs. Vianello walked over to the statue of Mary that sat in a niche in the kitchen. She removed the rosary beads that hung around the statue's neck, struck a match, and lit the small candle that sat at her feet. Then she grabbed the bottle of holy water and blessed Maggie, Leo, and finally herself.

"You must take it back; it is cursed."

The sulfur smell from the match lingered in the air, causing Maggie to cough a little. "Patty is very nice. She is no more a witch than you or me."

Mrs. Vianello crossed herself three times very quickly. "See, Maggie is already coughing. Leo, take that flower back."

"I'll get rid of it, Mama," he answered.

"No, it must be taken back to where it was given. The curse has to be returned or will sit upon our heads."

Maggie's eyes widened as she fought the urge to laugh, but she managed to keep her mouth shut. She could see how upset Leo's mother was, so she stated, "We will take it back, Mrs. Vianello, I promise. Once we return, we will pray the Rosary with you. I'm so sorry that I didn't know."

She kissed Maggie on both sides of her face. "Go quickly, child; night is settling in."

Mrs. Vianello watched from the doorway as Maggie and

Leo climbed into the small Ape. Once they were down the road a good bit, Leo burst out laughing. "My mom is the *most* superstitious woman in the world. Why didn't you tell me before we walked in the kitchen that you got that from Patty?"

"I didn't know that people actually believed it. But I made your mom a promise. We have to take it all the way back now."

Patty saw the small vehicle coming up the drive and laughed when she saw Maggie with the flower. "See, I told you so." Then she acknowledged Leo, "Hi Leo."

"I'm so sorry, Patty. How can we change this? How will people ever understand the truth?" Maggie asked, feeling so sad for her new friend. Then she had an idea, "Hey Patty, When's the last time you went to Mass?"

27

SUNDAY MASS

The church bells from Crista Rey tolled, summoning the island to Mass. The family packed into several vehicles, trying to make it to church on time. Maggie and Leo were in the Ape once again, but this time she relished their closeness, which was the only heat available in the vehicle. A slight mist fell on their windshield, a brutal companion to the cold; she eagerly awaited the warmth of the church.

They entered the small church, which was ordinarily gloomy but was surprisingly alive and cheery that day. There were live potted plants and trees scattered around the building and beautiful arrangements around the altar. It was such a transformation that the parishioners were a buzz, surveying each springtime selection and appreciating the life it brought into their parish on a cold winter's day. Maggie's grin spread across her face as she leaned in and whispered only one word to Leo, "Patty."

Father G celebrated Mass, and as always, his homily was

both relevant and inspiring. During the final announcements, he summoned everyone's attention and thanked the altar servers, eucharistic ministers, and musicians. Then he added, "Last, but certainly not least, I would like to thank our new florist and parishioner, Mrs. Patty Sprague." Everyone erupted in applause, but as Patty stood up, there was a deafening hush that spread across the small church. Father G continued, "Patty moved to our island a few years back. She and her husband were scientists who came to us from California. They were doing cancer research using native plants such as the mandrake. Her husband, Brett, was fighting a very advanced cancer. In an attempt to find a cure, he experimented with several different formulas. We all know the outcome of this; may he rest in peace, but many of you may not know the story behind it. Some have even come up with stories on your own." He paused briefly, giving the congregation time to reflect. He even stared down a few of the top gossipers. Then he continued, "We take care of each other on this island, so if you haven't had the opportunity to meet Patty, please introduce yourself after Mass."

As soon as Father G had processed out, Maggie went straight to Patty. She realized what a huge step Patty had taken and hoped the congregation would embrace her. One by one, as the parishioners exited the church, they introduced themselves to her as Father G protectively stood nearby. Everyone, including Patty, spoke in Italian, so Maggie could not follow the conversations well. After the last person walked by, Patty happily told Maggie that everyone had been very kind. She also said that she had two coffee invites, one lady was coming over for lunch, and the bee man wanted to have a heart-to-heart.

"Who is Mr. Beeman?"

"No, he is actually the man who keeps the bees on the island. His name is Stefano Moretto. He asked me over tomorrow night. Will you go with me? He makes me nervous."

"Absolutely, I'd love to. But in the meantime, if someone is coming to your house, I strongly suggest you move the baby plants off of your front porch. You don't want to freak anyone out before they step foot in the door."

"Ahh, the mandrake lookalikes are so cute, and they won't hurt a fly. They are my treasures."

"Well, I strongly suggest making them your buried treasures and getting them out of sight."

Patty laughed, saying, "No way!" and Maggie ended the conversation, "Way!"

28

THE BEEKEEPER

Maggie glanced at the kitchen clock, sipping the last of her Café Americano. "I'm going to be late. Patty is going to kill me," she said, jumping to her feet. She grabbed her coat and scarf from the inside peg and yelled goodbye over her shoulder.

Leo ran out behind her, "I'll walk you over." But he was struggling to keep up. "Do you always walk this fast?"

"I've got so much energy; I feel like I could fly. What was in that coffee?"

"Double espresso, just like always."

"Yep, that would do it. I try to drink half-caff. Sometimes caffeine gives me the jitters."

He got in sync with her quick pace and explained where she would be visiting that evening. "Moretto honey had been the sweetener for Venice's nobility for hundreds of years. You see, every person on Sant' Erasmus Island has a role. With only 700 people who reside here, we each play our part. The Moretto family are good people, and they keep our bees."

Leo made a buzzing noise and pinched the back of Maggie's arm. She saw it coming, but feigned a small yelp and then broke out into laughter. He smiled and continued to chase her down the path as Patty's house came into view.

Patty was pacing back and forth on her front porch as Maggie walked up. Her hair was pulled back and hung in controlled ringlets, and she wore just the right amount of make-up to enhance her beauty while looking natural. When she saw Maggie, she sighed, "I was so worried you forgot to come. Thank you so much."

Maggie said goodbye to Leo, then turned her attention to Patty. She gave her a hug hello, and they began walking to the Moretto country house. "So, how well do you know this beekeeper?"

"When we moved to the island, he was the first person we met. He was concerned that we might bring plants from the States that would affect his honey. He was right, you know." She shrugged her shoulders and took in a deep breath. "Some of our plants would have affected his honey, but we kept those flowers in the greenhouse, and I still do. The only plants growing outdoors are native plants to this area."

"Is he nice?"

"Well...., he wasn't nice or mean; he was all business. He came by every few months and always talked to Brett. He's only come by twice since his passing. I don't think he knows what to say to me."

As they approached the house, a man was sitting on the patio of the two-story apricot stucco house. Mr. Moretto was tanned by the sun and physically fit from the labor; he appeared to be a much younger man than he was. "Hmmm.

Is there a Mrs. Moretto?" she asked Patty and wagged her eyebrows. He was surprisingly nice-looking. Maggie had pictured the man being a toad after the way Patty had described him. She now understood why Patty's hair and make-up were fixed so perfectly. Maggie wondered if she had been hoodwinked.

Patty swatted her, speaking quietly but forcefully, "I might have overheard talk around town that his wife had passed away. But, the talk is never directed at me, so I'm unsure. Now behave, or I'll send you home early."

He stood as they approached and seemed surprised that Patty had brought Maggie. He was very kind and welcomed her, but he focused entirely on Patty.

Darkness had been chasing at their heels as they walked to his house. They were pleased when Mr. Moretto invited them straight inside to get out of the cold. He led them to a comfortable living room with a fireplace. The warm glow of a fire, and the sweet smell in the air, offered an inviting coziness that caused Maggie to let out a soft sigh.

The small sitting room was simple, with an exposed beam ceiling. Many pictures of bees and flowers hung on the beige plastered walls, reminding Maggie of similar prints hanging in Patty's cottage. As they settled into a tan linen sofa that seemed to give a hug, he brought out a tray. It was filled with different crackers, pretzels, and cheeses accompanied by different colored jars of honey. He then offered what appeared to be a glass of champagne. "This is dry sparkling mead, made from our honey."

Maggie spun the glass studying its contents. Noticing her hesitation, the beekeeper raised his glass in a silent toast, and they all took a sip. Maggie's "yum" made him smile.

"Mead is the oldest fermented beverage in the world, dating back to the Middle Ages. There was only mead until that greedy climbing grape vine stretched out its tendrils across Italy." Maggie took another sip and let the unmistakable flavor, with a hint of citrus, make its way across her tongue. Then, following his lead, she grabbed a cracker and a piece of cheese.

He broke their silence by saying, "Patty?" with such force that the two women jumped. His face blushed instantly, but he toned down his volume and tried again. "So, Patty, is your background in botany?"

"Yes, I graduated from Berkley with a plant biology major. I started working straight out of college for one of the largest producers of cut flowers in the States. They were located in the Santa Barbara area, Lompoc Valley to be exact."

"So, what is your favorite flower?"

Patty thought the question a test, so she began slowly and thoughtfully. "They have changed so many times in my life. Before I was married, it was the bird of paradise." Stefano nodded his head slowly in agreement. "But the chrysanthemum was my favorite flower for most of my life, until recently. These days, I have two that interchange most regularly; they are forget-me-nots and yarrow."

Patty and Stefano sat, transfixed on one another. Maggie looked from one to the other, wondering what she had missed. She knew that plants had different meanings, and she assumed that was what they were referring to, but she had no idea what information had just flown between them. Finally, Stefano cleared his throat. "Tell me, are you the one taking care of Father Misto...and his camellias?"

"Guilty as charged. The coffee grounds from my caffeine addiction, along with the holy soil around the church, have made his camellias the prettiest in Italy. As far as Father Misto himself, I do what I can to help him."

"Father G said your tea is the only thing that helps with his multiple sclerosis," Stefano stated.

"It's been harder and harder to find the evening primrose, but I go out most evenings with my lantern and continue to look." Maggie conjured the image of Patty standing on the side of the cliff with the lantern and felt guilty she judged Patty without knowing her.

"I'll keep a lookout for patches when I'm out and about on the island," Stefano said with a crooked smile. It was clear his intentions were romantic and not business, and Maggie felt awkward sitting between the flying sparks. She was happy when they were interrupted by his son, who had stopped by to pick up gear for a honey tour he was giving the following day. Maggie jumped at the opportunity to get away from the couple and begged the son for a ride back to the Vianello's home. Patty seemed to be enjoying Stefano and was completely happy for Maggie to leave.

As Maggie walked out the door, she looked back, and the two of them had moved closer to one another. The last thing she heard before closing the door was, "So Stefano, tell me everything about you...oh, and your honey, too."

29

LORETO

Over the next several weeks, Leo and Maggie fell into a comfortable routine. Every morning, once his family went to work in the covered fields, they would go over to the new business headquarters. There was much to be done before the tourist season began, so they started with the basics and worked their way up to the difficult. They transformed the loft to add an office. They were able to separate the space with makeshift wall dividers and keep a small bedroom. They fixed the street-side door to look like a business, and spent countless hours sprucing up the attached garden. The area would need several kayaks, so Leo built racks on the outside walls. The only thing missing were the kayaks themselves. Finding them for sale around Venice was impossible, but Leo located ten at a nearby resort. He was eager to see them firsthand, so they planned a trip to look them over.

They took the vaporetto to the Santa Lucia train station and walked to the waiting train. Maggie had only seen the sea-side areas around Venice, so she was excited as the train made its way across the countryside. The rolling hills dotted with red clay roofed houses were a stark contrast to the tall buildings around Venice.

The resort was located in Rimini, but when it was announced that Rimini was the next stop, Leo made no attempt to move. "Isn't this our stop?" she asked.

"We will come back to Rimini, but I thought we would go somewhere else first." After riding an hour more, the town of Loreto was announced.

"Loreto, where have I heard that before? Wait, that's from the posters in the back of Chiesa degli Scalzi," Maggie remarked.

Leo nodded. "I have wanted to take you there from the moment you mentioned seeing the posters in Venice. It is said to be the house from Nazareth of the Blessed Mother, Mary."

He pointed out the train window as the hillside town slowly came into view. "During the Crusades, Christians kept the Holy House safe in Nazareth. But when the Christians were defeated and returned home, the Holy House was left unguarded. God had other plans to keep it out of danger. Overnight, the house was moved." She looked at him quizzically and he nodded, "Yep, it was just picked up and moved. Whenever trouble came, the house was moved. Again and again, across land and sea. And people saw it happen. Some saw it pass overhead; some even saw it flown over the water by angels. Each move was made either because of a threat of destruction or to escape the greed of men. It has been safe in Loreto for seven hundred years. Historical and archaeological research now confirm that it is the house from Nazareth."

Maggie hung on to Leo's every word and hadn't realized she had been holding her breath until she inhaled a gulp of air.

Leo continued, "When I was on the water as a boy, I secretly watched for angels carrying the house, wondering if it could be moving again." He smiled, recollecting moments from his past.

As the train slowed, they made their way to the exit to step off before it went to the next stop. They took a taxi into the city and were dropped at the pathway to the basilica. Maggie immediately felt the pull on her calves as they walked up the hill. At one point, they stopped and looked over the countryside. Maggie was surprised to see water in the distance. Leo must have read her mind because he explained they were less than three miles from the Adriatic Sea.

They entered the large ornate doors and followed the line of pilgrims towards the back. The Holy House itself was encased inside an ivory marble shrine that was covered inside the basilica. It reminded Maggie of the Russian nesting dolls stacked one inside of the other. As she walked inside, a peaceful feeling set over her. She found herself wanting to stay as she slowly looked around the primitive stone house. The line of eager pilgrims was pushing her along, but her feet wouldn't move.

Leo watched the awe in her face and eventually grabbed her elbow and moved her to the corner. He pointed down to a glass section of the floor where she could see the original base, then he whispered in her ear, "It's the holiest place in the world."

As they were leaving, something made her linger in the back of the church. She had to walk through the house one more time. This time was done prayerfully, thanking Mary for the "yes" that she had given to be the mother of Christ.

Walking down the long side aisle leaving the church, she noticed the line of confessionals that flanked the sidewalls. Three of the four sat open with their curtains tied back, but the last one had a line with three people waiting. She thought about that night with Leo and joined them. Although she knew the final "Go and sin no more" would be difficult, she was truly sorry that she had chosen to spend the night with him. After being in such a holy place as Loreto, she knew it was not what God intended for her.

The cold air hit Maggie in the face as they stepped out of the church, and she cuddled into Leo's arm. They walked hand in hand back towards the car in silence, both deep in their own thoughts. Finally, Leo broke the silence. "When I was fourteen, my papa brought our family on pilgrimage to Loreto. It was a big deal. We shut down the farm, which we never did, and the whole family came. It changed me when I stood inside the house. At that very moment, I knew that I wanted a holy marriage.

"I was a hellion, but this trip settled me. Papa told us that God could have placed Jesus into this world with lots of wealth and splendor, but he chose to place him in a Holy Family. He said that he prayed that each of us would be blessed to find a holy spouse, as he had."

Maggie looked at Leo and smiled. She always loved the Holy Family, but had never thought of searching for a holy spouse. It all made sense now. "Your papa was amazing, Leo."

"Yes, he was. And so are you. The day I saw you in your backyard on Tybee, and you explained the Holy Family birdbath, I knew you were unique. But seeing you find peace inside the Holy House today confirms it. You're special, Maggie. I hope you know how amazing I think you are."

Maggie blushed deeply. Being acknowledged for her love of something holy embarrassed her. It made her worry he saw something that wasn't there. She didn't feel holy at all; she felt unworthy. She had a lump in her throat the size of a baseball and tried very hard to control her emotions. "Thank you for bringing me here. I will never, ever forget it," she said as she reached up and kissed his cheek.

THE TRAIN MADE its way back to the Rimini stop. Maggie was deep in thought when the ocean came into view, causing her to snap to attention to get a better view of the beach. She opened her window and took in the smell of the salt air. The icy cold air left a sting in her nose, and the passengers around her shot angry glances her way as they bundled into their coats. The tracks ran parallel to the coast. It reminded her of driving along Butler Avenue on Tybee. The houses, restaurants, and small hotels sat between the road and the beach. She smiled, once again, amazed at the similarities between coastal Georgia and northern Italy and felt a tug on her heart for home.

Darkness fell upon them. Although it was barely five o'clock, it felt much later. Leo laughed as her stomach growled out loud, so after they checked into the Hotel Bellevue and put their luggage in the room, they went in search of dinner. Leo pulled her into Lella's, a cute restaurant on the promenade. They were seated at a table by the window and were given placemats that doubled as menus. Maggie looked down, and the word "hamburger" caught her attention. She was so excited she told the waitress right away that she wanted the hamburger. Leo did the same.

Maggie eagerly awaited her burger. She hadn't realized how much she had missed American food until that moment and pictured the big juicy burger from the Crystal Beer Parlor. As the waitress placed the burger's distant Italian cousin in front of her on the table, Maggie said, "Hello, old friend. I've missed you so!" The waitress called it hamburger piates, a very thin patty wrapped in flatbread. But Maggie's taste buds were in heaven as she took a bite. It was just the touch of America that she needed.

"Have you been terribly homesick during your weeks here?" Leo asked.

"Not exactly homesick, but I do miss the pace of Savannah, seeing people every day I grew up with, and the feeling of security. I especially miss my friends. I've talked to each of them a couple of times, but it's powerful when we are all together at lunch. But Sant' Erasmus feels very home-like. Probably being on the water every day has helped with that, too. What about you when you were in Savannah?"

"I love Tybee. If I didn't have things hanging over my head, I might not have ever left."

His statement made Maggie smile. "If you didn't have things hanging over your head, I might not have let you."

He leaned in closer, "Oh yeah? Why's that?"

She leaned in to meet him, "Because...by the end of the summer...you were the most requested kayak instructor." She laughed, slowly backing away from him. "Everyone wanted lessons from the Savannah Gondolier."

He leaned back into his chair, "Well, you never know, do you? They might still get the chance."

They had an early morning appointment with the Hotel Bellevue to inspect the kayaks the following day. By the end of the meeting, Leo had brought his family a sizable new produce customer while at the same time purchasing the last supplies needed to begin his business. Several days later, the kayaks were shipped on the boat the Bellevue sent to pick up their produce from Sant' Erasmus.

30

SHOE ON THE OTHER FOOT

L eo had a meeting with the council to review his permits and hopefully set a date to open his business. He asked Maggie to ride to Venice with him. She waited in a small trattoria known for its Italian-style mulled wine, vin brulé. She had just taken her first sip of the warm, cinnamon-flavored wine when a man walked up and motioned to the adjacent chair to join her.

"*No, grazie*," she said, waving him off with her free hand, but he continued to sit.

"I'm a gondolier and a friend of Leo's. May I sit with you?"

Well, you're already sitting, so do you really care? she thought as she forced a smile.

Although he smiled back, it never quite reached his eyes. The eyes always gave it away. Maggie didn't recognize the man and introduced herself, and he did the same, saying his name was Michael. He commented on her drink, nodding with approval, but quickly questioned her ability to handle its high alcohol content. He called the waitress over and ordered the same drink and a charcuterie board that was brought almost immediately. It held a wide variety of cheeses, salami, nuts, dates, and a pear.

"Please, eat," he said and motioned to the food. "Tell me, how is it that Leo left you all alone today?"

The way he had asked made her feel defensive, as if Leo had done something wrong, but she answered honestly. "He has a big meeting to look over all of his business permits and licenses with the city council."

"So, it is true then, Leo is leaving the gondoliers? I thought he loved what he did and was just taking a break."

"I think he does, but things haven't been the same since his dad's death."

She noticed a far-off look in his eyes, so she asked him how long he'd known Leo, but his mind was somewhere else, and he never answered her question. All of a sudden, Michael's attention came back to her and he asked, "How is he dealing with things. Is he getting over it? It's been like a year now, right?" He knew how long it had been, down to the minute of the day, but he wasn't letting her know.

His questions made her feel very protective of Leo, so she changed things around and decided to answer questions with questions, hoping for the correct answers. "Are you close to your dad, Michael?"

"Yes, my papa and I are close."

That was the exact answer she was looking for, so she dug a little further, "Very close?"

This time, he just nodded as he locked eyes with Maggie. His glare stopped her for a second, but she continued. "Now picture your father dying the way Leo's dad did."

Michael saw firsthand how Leo's dad died and couldn't imagine if that had been his own father. His eyes instantly stung at the thought, but the woman continued to talk. Damn her. He wanted to flee from the table, but he was frozen by her stare. "Then, as you and your family's hearts are breaking apart, there is no sympathy from others; there is only scandal. And to make matters worse, some of the people you've worked with your whole life turn their backs on you."

Michael stared at her with complete hate, daring her to finish her assault. "I know nothing about you or your relationship with Leo, but here's what I do know. I've been in Italy for seven weeks, and I haven't been introduced to you, or any other gondolier for that matter. So, I think it's safe to say that you are not the friend that you claim to be. But to answer your question, Leo is finding a new path to his happiness."

Michael broke her gaze just in time to see Leo making his way to the restaurant entrance. Looking down at Maggie, he quickly stood and said, "Thanks for your honesty. You do not mince words. It was both unnerving and enlightening. Leo is lucky to have found you. *Buona sera*." Then he threw money on the table and walked towards the rear of the building.

Maggie watched Michael's back as he walked away. She was unsettled after their odd and abrupt conversation, but she couldn't put her finger on the reason why. There was definitely more to this Michael character than she was aware. Her eyes fell to the uneaten charcuterie board. She popped a date in her mouth just as Leo appeared at the table.

Holding a small bouquet of flowers out to her, he said, "All the permits are complete, and we have an opening date. We can open our doors for business on March 17th."

She jumped from the table and into his arms. All of their hard work was finally paying off. But March 17th? St. Patrick's Day was such a big day in Savannah. Practically the whole city went to the parade. Over and above that, it was one of the biggest tourist days. She was already booked solid the week before and after. The time was coming quickly to make some big decisions. Had she accomplished what she had come to Venice to do? Her return airline ticket was dated February 26th, but her heart was tugging her to stay with Leo.

31

TRUTH

Michael walked into the empty kitchen. When was the last time his mom had cooked? Memories flooded his mind of coming home as a boy and his mother being in the kitchen. He called out to her, "Ma? Ma, you home? Is there anything here to eat?" His words hung in the air. He was surprised when she came around the corner.

She hadn't changed much from his boyhood memories. Her hair didn't show a strand of grey, and her face was smooth and wrinkle-free. But somehow, he no longer recognized her as the mother he once knew, making him wonder if he ever really knew her at all.

"You need to find a wife who will cook for you," she said, leaving the smell of cigarette smoke hanging in the air. He looked into her cold eyes as she spoke. Had they always been that way, and he hadn't noticed? And when had she started smoking? Had he been so involved with his own problems that he didn't see the transformation of his mother?

"I'm going out," she told him as she straightened the bodice of her form-fitting long black dress. In doing so, the deep V neckline plunged further down. Michael winced and diverted his eyes.

"Where is Papa? Is he going with you?" he asked.

Her cold laugh told it all. "Heavens no. Your father is an embarrassment at events like these."

She glanced at the large book beneath Michael's arm. "What have you got there?" she asked.

"Aunt Mita made this for me. Take a look." Michael opened a large scrapbook with a navy-blue leather cover and started flipping the pages.

Monica casually flipped through the first two pages then slammed it shut. "She should spend more time living her own life then clipping articles about yours," she said. Then she walked towards the door. "Don't wait up!" she called out over her shoulder and slammed the door behind her.

Michael was left swimming in an ocean of perfume and clove cigarettes, and he quickly moved to an open space to escape. Rooting around the kitchen, he found a loaf of bread that wasn't too stale. Slicing it down the middle, he spread some tomato sauce on each half, added thick slices of mozzarella cheese, and put it in the oven. He sliced tomatoes and cucumbers, sat down at the table, and waited on the makeshift pizza. It would be just enough for him and his dad.

He looked around the kitchen once more, thinking back to when he was a boy. There were always fresh groceries in the house, and a meal was prepared every afternoon. When had that stopped? He dug back a little deeper into his memory. His mom was always in the kitchen, but his father was always wearing an apron. Had Michael always given credit to his mother for his father's efforts? Then memories started flooding in. He couldn't recall one memory of quality time with just his mother. His dad always did the work: cooking, cleaning, or playing with him while his mom took all the credit. His dad was so kind that he didn't need the praise.

Michael slammed his hand down hard onto the table, cursing his stupidity. He had taken advice from a very selfish woman. He had tortured himself for the last year, and she didn't care at all. She only cared about herself. Then he thought about his conversation with Leo's girl, Maggie, and knew what he had to do.

MITA CLOSED her eyes as the morning bells began to toll. She squeezed her hands, still remembering the feel of the course rope against her fingers. It had been her job to ring the bells; the job was always given to a postulant at Suore Canossiane Convent in Cannaregio. "Wake up. Wake up, Venice. It's seven o'clock. Mass will begin soon," she muttered just as she had done every morning.

Once the seventh ring fell silent, she tried to get back to work, but she couldn't stop thinking about her visit with Michael. He had seemed so downhearted the day before when he stopped in for a visit, but seemed to cheer up when she gave him the scrapbook. She wondered how she could help him. As if her thoughts had conjured his presence, she jumped when she noticed him at the door.

"I was sitting on the bench waiting to see movement in

the shop. I know you were waiting on the bells," Michael said.

Mita smiled at the boy she loved so well. "The church tells me when to begin my day. I never open before seven."

"Yes, I know your schedule," he replied as he helped her move her sidewalk plants out the door.

Mita noticed his tired eyes. "Are you well? You look tired."

"I'm fine. I just didn't sleep well," Michael answered but then decided to be truthful. "Actually, I'm struggling. I've done something I'm not very proud of, and I think the time has come to make things right."

Mita grabbed hold of his hand and squeezed until his eyes met hers. "Is this big secret the thing that has kept you so worried the past few months?" Michael nodded, so she asked another question. "Is it illegal?"

"No, Aunt Mita. But it will hurt the people around me. Still, I must tell the truth."

"Yes, you must." She stood on her tiptoes and reached her arms around his neck for a long hug. Pulling back, she looked him in the eyes. "God will take care of you, and your aunt Mita will love you no matter what." He kissed her cheek and ran out the glass door.

"Oh, Michael, you sweet boy," she muttered. It sickened her that Monica had encouraged Michael to lie about the accident. How could a mother think so little of her child? Mita fumed with anger. She must do something to help him. She walked to her desk and pulled out the ledger where she had kept track of all of Monica's dealings. There were many pages full of names. She had also written her assumptions off to the side. She scanned down to the current entries and narrowed her eyes at the name she had written beside March 10th. It was the same man found floating in the canal the morning prior. It could be just a coincidence, but who's to say? She closed her eyes, calculating the consequences, but all she could see was Michael's saddened face. Circling March 10th with a red pen, she shoved the ledger into an envelope and wrote Mr. Bianco's name across the front.

MICHAEL WAITED in the park across from Mr. Bianco's office. When his father untied the gondola and made his way down the canal, Michael knocked on the door.

Mr. Bianco's assistant, Sergio, answered and knew who he was. Sergio made it his business to know anyone of importance in Venice. After inviting Michael into the foyer, he asked, "To what do we owe the honor? Do we have a meeting with the future premiere gondolier?"

"No, I do not have a scheduled meeting, but I must speak to Mr. Bianco. It's a matter of utmost urgency."

"Mr. Bianco has a full schedule, but I could squeeze you in early next week."

Michael began nodding his head in agreement. He had waited this long; what would a few days matter? Out of the corner of his eye, he saw movement and noticed it was Mr. Bianco. He came and stood right in front of Michael, and Sergio began his formal introduction. "Mr. Bianco, may I introduce you to Michael Vianello, the future private gondolier for the Bianco family."

Mr. Bianco took Michael's hand into both of his, "Michael, it's very nice to meet you. We will one day be very close friends, just like your father and I have become. Please, have breakfast with me."

Michael understood the chain of command and immediately looked to Sergio for approval before agreeing. Sergio gave a very slight nod, and Michael agreed. The fireplace was burning bright as they entered Mr. Bianco's private office and sat at a small round table overlooking the canal. A waiter quickly added another place setting and poured both men a cup of coffee.

Mr. Bianco began, "I have been visited by many men in this city asking for many things; favors, money, and power. Tell me, Michael, what is it you ask of me on this cold morning in March?" Michael appreciated how this man of great wealth got right down to business before Michael even took the first sip of his coffee. "I need to tell you a story."

That got Mr. Bianco's attention, and he sat up attentively. "Continue, please."

Michael told him about the day he witnessed the accident. He told him how he rushed to Claudio, but was too late and how distraught he was because he greatly respected Claudio and admired his kindness. Lastly, he explained going home covered in blood and his mother convincing him to lie to the police. He finally took the first sip of his now cold coffee when he finished.

Mr. Bianco inhaled a deep breath and exhaled loudly, saying, "God rest Claudio's soul." He looked over at Sergio, who was stunned quiet, then said out loud, "Who knows of this story?"

"Only the priest at Santa Maria Gloriosa dei Frari."

"Not even your papa?"

"Most of all, not my papa. He is an innocent victim here."

"Why are you coming to me now? Everything is running just as you planned."

"Not as I planned. I was in shock and told one lie that has changed many lives. My conscience can't take it anymore. I'm ready to suffer the consequences and get on with my life. My Papa respects you; he is a hard worker, devoted husband, and father. My mom, well, that's another story. I'm very, very sorry, Mr. Bianco."

"Thank you for your honesty. Things will be exactly as they are supposed to be. Go now, and do not mention a word of this to anyone."

The two men stood, and Mr. Bianco walked around the table to Michael. He put his hands on each side of Michael's face. "You've done the right thing, Michael. Now you must let this go so that you can start living again." To his surprise, Michael reached up and immediately hugged the older gentleman, but he was even more surprised when Mr. Bianco hugged him back.

32

HOMELESS

Sergio escorted Michael to the door and stood in the foyer as Michael tried to regain his composure. Michael's family had been the Biancos' gondoliers for centuries. Sergio was close to his grandfather and now was close to his father, Pietro. Sergio thought back to that morning 25 years ago when Michael's grandfather didn't wake up. As soon as Sergio had received word, he immediately asked Pietro to an early morning meeting and was surprised that he had brought his new bride, Monica, with him.

The couple had been seated in Mr. Bianco's lavish living room by 7:15 a.m. Sergio got right to the point, "Do you hold a license, and have you finalized your training to become the Biancos' private gondolier?"

Pietro began, "My father's license was to be passed to me, but I have not finished my__"

Sergio interrupted, "Do you understand that without

completion of your training, you can-not be the gondolier for the Biancos?"

Pietro answered, "I do understand, but I'm very close to_"

Sergio cut him off once again. "The Biancos are very sorry to hear the news of your father's passing." He paused with respect, then finished, "However, there can never be a moment when the Bianco family does not have access to a private gondolier. The commerce of Venice depends on this."

Monica blurted out, "We would like to speak with Mr. Bianco." Both her husband and Sergio looked at her with surprise, so she quickly added, "We'll wait." And wait they did, for almost two hours while Monica paced.

When Mr. Bianco entered the room, he walked straight to Pietro and engulfed him in a warm hug. When they parted, Mr. Bianco was in tears, "I loved your father as if he were my brother. The world was a much better place with him in it." Only then did Pietro let out a gut-wrenching cry. He had been so consumed with worry about the family's future; he hadn't let his brain acknowledge the loss of his father. Completely crushed, he sat down on the sofa and buried his head in his hands. Monica sat beside him but didn't touch him.

Mr. Bianco pulled a leather armchair to sit directly across from him and placed his hand on Pietro's shoulder, "I'm so sorry, Pietro," he said and let the young man cry.

When Pietro was done, Mr. Bianco pulled a handkerchief from his pocket, sat up tall, and began, "For centuries, your family has been the private gondoliers for mine. I know this is hard for you, but since you're not ready, this tradition now rests on the shoulder of your uncle, Claudio."

Monica had flown to her feet. "How dare you! Pietro is so close to obtaining his license. If you truly loved his father, as you claim, then you would give him time to finish."

Sergio appeared out of thin air and quickly stood between Mr. Bianco and Monica. Looking her squarely in the eyes, he firmly said, "*Never* speak to Mr. Bianco this way, especially in his own home." Monica narrowed her eyes at Sergio and slowly sat back down.

Mr. Bianco ignored her entirely and continued to speak directly to Pietro. "I didn't make these family laws, but I must adhere to them. I must have a licensed gondolier in place by sundown. I will promise you this; if any hardship or disgrace ever comes upon our next gondolier, your family will be our immediate choice. Sergio will put it in writing. And if you ever need me, you know how to get in touch." Then he stood, kissed Pietro on both cheeks, and left.

After 25 years, Sergio could still picture the grief in Pietro's eyes and thought about how Michael's confession would destroy the man. He was startled when Mr. Bianco touched his arm and brought him back to the present. "Once again, my friend, you were right about Monica. All those years ago, you sensed something was different about her, then reiterated it last year when Pietro called for a meeting the day of Claudio's accident. I'm sorry I didn't listen to you."

"I'm sorry I was right. Monica throws a big wake, and she has now hurt many. I worry that there are still many things unanswered about her. The snake may have been exposed; it still roams free."

"Let's put a tail on her for a while. I want to know her every move." Mr. Bianco continued, processing the recent information out loud. "Pietro is a good man. The news of his son lying by order of his mother will kill him." He closed his eyes, shook his head, and loudly exhaled. "When Pietro came in last year, he could hardly speak. He simply handed me the paper stating that Pietro Vianello could be reinstated as the Biancos' gondolier if any disgrace fell upon Claudio Vianello. He looked pained, handing it to me, and his humility touched me. We have much to consider. What do you know of Claudio's son, Leo? Do you know where he resides?"

Sergio nodded, knowing exactly where Leo had been keeping his days and with whom. His job was to know these things, even if Monica Vianello had fallen between the cracks.

"Then let us pay him a visit. Let's go for a walk, Sergio; I won't be taking the gondola today."

Now that they had an official opening date, Leo was excited to hang signs on both sides of the new office to let people know of his new business. He had decided to name his company Venice Adventure Kayaks, VAK for short. Maggie had happily agreed and offered to design a metal sign to hang along the canal and a lovely wooden sign to hang streetside.

After fighting with the old, exposed concrete on the canal, they finally secured the sign to the side of the door where all boat traffic could see it. When they walked to the front of the building to hang the second sign, Maggie noticed two men sitting on a bench, hovering under a large wool blanket. She had become accustomed to seeing homeless people on the street. However, it was unusually cold outside, and she felt sad to know they didn't have anywhere warm to retreat. While Leo bothered with the sign, Maggie ran inside and poured two hot cups of coffee, grabbed two chunks of panettone Leo's mother had made that morning, and carried it straight to the freezing men.

The men looked startled to see her approach, so she started jabbering to put them at ease. "It sure is chilly this morning. I thought you might want something to warm your bellies after spending the night on this cold bench. I brought you some coffee and panettone."

Sergio angrily jumped to his feet to defend Mr. Bianco's honor, but Mr. Bianco patted his arm to sit back down. The thick brown blanket draped across them had fallen to the ground, and Maggie noticed their three-piece business suits and gold jewelry. She blushed deeply. "Oh my gosh, I'm so sorry. I didn't know you were...you were...you are definitely NOT homeless."

Leo noticed the commotion and walked up behind her. He recognized Mr. Bianco immediately and quickly stepped in, "Mr. Bianco, I'm so sorry. Maggie has been taking care of the people on the streets since she arrived in Venice. No offense intended."

Leo was shocked when Mr. Bianco addressed him directly, "Hello, Leo." Then he nodded at Maggie, "Nice to meet you, Maggie. They say a truly good-hearted person treats all people equally, whether they live on the street or own the street. Thank you for your kindness." He reached over and took the coffee and cake from her hands. Shivering, he turned to Leo, "May we speak to you, preferably inside?"

Leo led the men into the office and directed them to the

small table in the kitchen. Mr. Bianco got right to the point. "This conversation must stay between us for the time being, but Leo, I'd also like for you to tell your mother; God knows she has been through enough. Please let Rosa know I will take care of everything." Everybody nodded in agreement.

Mr. Bianco told them about Michael's visit. When he explained the truth about Leo's father's accident, Leo stood up quickly. He walked to the large window overlooking the canal. His tears unwillingly fell down his face, but he continued listening intently. Mr. Bianco told them about Monica and the deception and that Pietro was totally unaware of the situation. Then, he made his final statement. "The position is open to you if you would like it. Pietro would be happy to cut back to part-time until he retires in a couple of years. Only you can tell us how this ends."

Mr. Bianco stood. "I honor my gondolier once a year on Shrove Tuesday at Carnivale. Can you give me your answer before it begins?"

Leo nodded and, looking him in the eye, said, "Yes, I will let you know. Thank you for delivering this message in person." Mr. Bianco patted Leo's shoulder twice, gave his respects to Maggie, and left quietly out the streetside door.

Maggie had followed the men to the door and shut it behind them. She started to giggle, "Oh my gosh, I thought they were homeless." But when she noticed the far-off look in Leo's eyes, she stopped talking.

"The job is open to me," he muttered in a daze. Maggie was shocked by his interest when he went on, "I'd be a fool if I turned it down. It's a dream job."

Maggie's heart dropped, and her stomach tightened. She had heard that statement before. "It's my dream job." Trevor had said those exact four words. In her mind, dream jobs trump everything and everyone else. Worry settled into her chest, but her thoughts were interrupted by Leo's voice.

"We need to get home. Mama needs to know," he said and gathered his things.

They found his mom making lunch, so Leo asked her to sit with him at the kitchen table. He took her hand into his and told her the whole story. Mrs. Vianello didn't react, nor did she wipe the tears that fell softly down her face and into her lap. When Leo was finished, she simply stood up and walked out the door.

She took the path to the shoreline and watched the clouds creep across the lagoon and slowly overtake Venice, just like they had on the day of Claudio's death. She slowly began her prayer for Claudio's safety, the one she had said every day of their marriage. She now realized this would be the last time.

"Dear Saint Erasmus, protector of all seamen. Thank you for guiding Claudio's gondola to the shore of his salvation. I pray, in Jesus' name, Amen."

As she said her final "Amen," she saw the flash of blue: Saint Elmo's Fire.

Mrs. Vianelli didn't realize Leo and Maggie had followed her to the coast. When the glow from the electrical charge left the sky, she heard a gasp behind her. She turned and reached out her hands to them with a smile, motioning them closer.

She had felt her grief lifting while she said the prayer to St. Erasmus, but the flash of light had given her the reassurance she needed. She knew the good Saint had interceded on Claudio's behalf. She had carried such sorrow over Claudio's death for so long; it was uplifting to say goodbye.

Mrs. Vianelli wrapped Leo and Maggie into a tight hug. As she slowly released them, she said, "Claudio can now rest well." She wiped a tear from Leo's face and then her own. "No more tears," she demanded. "Now come. Lunch won't fix itself." The three of them walked back, arm in arm. They laughed when the mist turned into rain, and they hurried back to the house. It was Claudio's gentle reminder that it was finally time to start laughing again.

That night, after dinner, Leo asked Maggie to sit with him outside in the garden. Unknowingly, Leo sat in his father's chair, and Maggie had sat in his mamas. "I need to talk to you about Mr. Bianco's offer. I know it probably sounds crazy to you, but I think I'm going to say yes. It really is a dream job."

Maggie placed her head into her hands, wondering how in the world she was in the exact same situation she had been with Trevor. She took her time to straighten, then spoke softly. "I can see this is a dream job. But is this your dream?"

He looked at her questioningly, then kept talking, completely ignoring her question. "Mr. Bianco is a very good man, and I would be making a nice income. I could buy a nice home and be able to start a family." He paused and took in a large gulp of air. Narrowing his gaze on Maggie, "Would you consider staying? Could you live in Venice?"

Maggie nervously looked around the porch, searching for something to focus on. A flashback to a conversation between her and Trevor played out in her mind. It was the week before she graduated from Georgia Southern, and she was telling him of the three out-of-town job offers she had received. "Would you consider staying in Savannah...with me?" he had asked, and she had. She moved home, worked downtown, and waited for him. And what had that given her...heartache. She wouldn't let her heart be broken again. Praying that she would come up with the correct response to Leo, she decided to just be honest. "As much as I love Venice, Savannah is my home, and that's where my dream job waits for me."

He took her hand and began to rub the top of hers with his thumb. Attempting to persuade her, he said, "You would love living in Venice. We could fix up the other side of the building and make it a very nice home, a place to raise a family. You could run the kayak company, just like you do the one on Tybee." He continued talking, but her brain stopped listening. Was he asking her to marry him? She wasn't sure of anything anymore.

Finally, she spoke. "Leo, this is your decision. This should not be based on me. One thing I know is that life is short and that you should never waste it doing something you do not love. You have to decide if this job is something that's going to make you happy." She stood up, kissed him softly on the lips, and left him sitting in the garden deep in thought.

Mrs. Vianello heard the kitchen door shut and looked down into the garden from her bedroom window. She was surprised to see Leo sitting in the same chair Claudio once sat upon. Reading his face, she could see he was troubled; a mama always knows. She liked Maggie. She was good for Leo and fit right into their family, but they had many obstacles ahead. She said a prayer for the couple and hoped that they would find every happiness that she and Claudio had once had.

MAGGIE IMMEDIATELY KNEW something was wrong as Mrs. Vianello shook her awake. "Maggie, wake up."

She opened her eyes to darkness and the rapid beat of her heart, "What's wrong?" she asked quickly.

"It's your father. He needs you to call him."

Maggie grabbed her cell phone that had been set to silent. The time read three in the morning, and she had four missed calls from her dad. Mrs. Vianello turned the bedside lamp on and walked slowly toward the door, wringing her hands.

Her dad answered on the first ring, "Maggie, thank God you called," he said before his voice cracked.

"What, Dad? What's happened?"

"Your mom. We didn't want to worry you, but she's been having severe shoulder pain. They scheduled her for angioplasty this morning. Somehow, during the procedure, they burst an artery. So they are doing surgery right now," he paused. Maggie knew he was trying to keep his emotions intact. But when he added, "I need you," the desperation came out in his voice, and he began to cry.

"I'm coming, Daddy. I'll be there as fast as I can." She didn't remember ending the call; she just started packing right away. Mrs. Vianello must have woken Leo because he was immediately at her side wanting to help. She was on a mission, not thinking, not feeling, just moving. It was Leo who made her stop and talk things through. "Why don't you jump in the shower. I'll call and get you on the next flight out. Mama is making you something to eat." Then he wrapped her in his arms, "I'm so sorry, Maggie."

It wasn't until the hot water hit her back that she lost it. She had kept her mom at arm's length for so long. What if she didn't make it through the surgery? Maggie might never get the chance to tell her she loved her. She prayed it wasn't too late.

Leo got her the last seat on the 7:30 a.m. flight to Atlanta. She would be in Savannah by that afternoon. He tried to talk to her several times on the drive to the airport, but she was only focused on making her flight and gave one-word responses. He walked her into the airport, and as they approached the security gate, he turned her to him. He began to speak, but she put her finger over his mouth. "I want only the best for you, Leo. I mean that. You deserve nothing less." She gently placed both hands on each side of his unshaven face and kissed him goodbye. She quickly turned and got into the security line, wiping the tears from her face.

He watched her make her way through security. "You are taking my heart back with you to Savannah. Our story is not over," he said quietly as he continued to watch her walk down the long airport terminal. Eventually, it swallowed her, and she was out of sight.

33

CORONARITAS

Caught in the alternate universe of hospital time, when a day feels like a week and an hour feels like a minute, Maggie's first week back in the States was a blur. Thankfully, her mom was recovering better than expected and was scheduled to be released from the hospital the following day. Maggie followed a florist delivery man down the hallway. She admired the blossoming yellow roses he was carrying. She smiled when he turned into her mother's room. Approaching the room, she slowed as the man exited, then paused in the doorway.

When her mother asked who had sent the flowers, her father handed the card to Victoria, who read it silently and commented, "Oh, isn't that nice? He sent flowers."

"Yeah, yeah. As if five dozen wasn't enough," her dad spit out. But as Maggie opened the door, the conversation ended. She couldn't wait to see who the flowers were from and finally got her chance when her dad went to dinner.

All the cards were the same, "Praying for your recovery. With love, James." Maggie quickly moved away from arrangements before being caught. Why would Trevor's dad send flowers? And so many, at that. Was there something that she didn't know about? Not so long ago, she would have just asked her dad, but things were still a little shaky between the two of them. Since she had come home, he continued to apologize about Trevor. She told him that she forgave him, but forgetting was more difficult.

The following day, her mom was released from the hospital with a heart-shaped pillow, a spirometer, and orders to de-stress her life. The last order was the one that Maggie worried most about because her mother had always thrived under pressure. Maggie tried to help as much as she could around the house. Even so, she quickly realized how much her parents relied on one another, and she was struggling to fill the gap of her mother's open role. She was happy when Wednesday finally rolled around and was excited to see all of her friends at their regular lunch.

The Mexican restaurant jumped to the beat of the perpetually festive street songs as Maggie searched for her friends. The tribe screamed when they saw her, and all got up from the table to greet her. It had been over two months, but they were so close that she didn't feel like she had missed anything. Sometimes, Savannah felt like a time warp, moving slowly like honey out of a jar.

They made it to the table, where everyone began talking at once while they fought for their turn to dip their chip into the salsa. Maggie's eyes got big when the waiter brought six large Coronaritas to the table. "What? You girls didn't order a drink? These six are for me, right?"

"God knows you need them," Agnes said while patting Maggie's back. "We sure did miss you."

This was their favorite Mexican restaurant, mainly because of their Coronarita drinks. It was a regular salted margarita with a Corona beer turned upside down in the glass. The fact that the beer didn't empty into the margarita amazed the group. But the funniest part was watching who would bump their glass first, breaking the pressure seal and causing the beer to empty out. That person would be forced to chug their drink.

"So, how's your mom?" Jan asked.

"She's healing great. The doctor said she should be back to normal in two-to-three weeks. But, you wanna hear something bizarre?" Everyone nodded around the table. "My parents truly love each other. Who would have thought, right? Maybe they always have, and I just didn't see it. It's funny what stepping into their everyday life and basically living there over the last week has taught me."

Stephanie asked, "Like what?"

"Like, my dad hasn't consumed a drop of alcohol for over ten years, and I had no idea. Every time I visited him at the bar, I thought he was drunk, but he was just hanging with his buds. Kinda like an old fart's coffee club...at a bar. Weird, I know. Also, my parents cannot work anything electrical; phones, microwaves, and especially the TV. Oh, and my mom is thinking about retiring. Yes, workaholic and 'nurse of the year', Victoria, might retire. *And*, I think I have been wrong about my parents over the last twenty years."

The table fell quiet as tears brimmed in Maggie's eyes. Each person was thinking about their own relationship with their parents. Finally, Latrice began, "I think we all have hit the point in our lives where we have adult relationships with our parents. It's crazy, getting older."

Silence fell upon the table until Maggie stood up. "Our parents might be getting older, but we sure aren't." Then she made eye contact with the waiter. "Another round," she yelled across the restaurant while all her friends waved her off. Still, another round was delivered, whether wise or not.

Gradually, the tribe started leaving one by one until only Maggie and Kathleen were left. Several half-drunk beverages were scattered around the table; however, Maggie wouldn't let the waiter clear. "I didn't want to pry, but...who am I kidding? I'm dying to know. How is Leo?" Kathleen asked. Maggie beamed at the mention of his name. "Ooh, that smile tells it all. Fill me in."

Maggie started from the beginning, explaining every-thing between her and Leo and how much she loved Venice. As she talked, she slowly finished each of the drinks left on the table. When she finally told Kathleen about her last week in Italy, she started stumbling over her words. "He asked me to stay. He wants me to live in Venice...with him." She put her elbows on the table to hold up her head which felt very heavy. "He makes me so happy. That should simply be enough." She laid her head onto the bend of her arm and stopped talking.

Kathleen looked at the empty glasses that Maggie had finished and then glanced around at her fellow patrons. She made eye contact with a lone man sitting at the bar who held up his margarita in a cheers motion. Kathleen shrugged and turned her attention back to Maggie. Had she fallen asleep right there at the table? She softly patted Maggie's back, who let out a small grunt in protest. "Why am I so scared?" she mumbled into her arm.

"Because love is a leap of faith. And let's face it, you leaped before and got hurt. Sometimes we just have to turn things over to God with an open heart; He always knows what's best for us," Kathleen answered. Then she glanced down at her watch, which read 2:15 and quickly began to gather her things. Her children were dismissed from school every day at 3:00; leaving at that moment would still put her in the very back of the carpool line. She gave Maggie a slight shake to get her head off the table and added, "Hey, my kids are gonna kill me if they are the last ones on the curb at carpool. I need to get going. I'll give you a lift home."

Kathleen helped Maggie into the kitchen door of her parent's house. She smiled, remembering all of the times they had snuck in that same door over the years. They were surprised to find Maggie's parents sitting at the kitchen table, watching them try to get inside with Maggie's arm draped over Kathleen. The girls stood frozen, like deer caught in headlights until Maggie burst out laughing.

Taking one look at their daughter, who was wearing the restaurant's happy birthday sombrero, which she had begged the young waiter to let her take home, they turned to Kathleen, "Kathleen Kenny, tell us right now. What's going on?"

It was Kathleen's turn to laugh out loud, "No one has called me by my maiden name in years," but she reverted back to being sixteen years old. "I'm happy to see you're recuperating well, Mrs. Martin. Nice to see you, Mr. Martin." She cleared her throat and acknowledged the reprimand.

"What happened? Coronaritas, that's what happened, and I think that Maggie might have been overserved."

Maggie steadied herself into one of the kitchen chairs. Kathleen watched Maggie sitting happily with her fiesta attire while her mom held her heart pillow to her chest. Kathleen blurted out, "I've got to run and pick up my kids from school; good to see you both," and made a quick retreat to the door.

Maggie and her parents sat at the small kitchen table. Her dad made coffee and brought a cup to Maggie. "Looks like you had fun at lunch. How's the tribe doing?" he asked.

"I really missed them while I was in Italy," Maggie murmured. She took a large sip of the bitter coffee, which slowly brought her towards sobriety. Noticing the travel brochures scattered around the table, she gathered them into a small stack.

Her mom motioned her head towards the brochures. "I think your father has finally talked me into retiring. The doctors say I need to de-stress my life, and I'll never be able to do that running the ER nurses. As soon as I get my release, your dad and I are going to travel a bit."

"Your mom and I have saved up a good amount of money to enjoy our future," her dad added. "I think the future is gonna start now. We plan to see the world. Then, when we are tired of the adventure, we will be back home."

Her mom interrupted, "Speaking of being tired, I think I'm going to take a nap." She gave Maggie a peck on the top of her head, then gave her dad a very long kiss. Maggie turned her head, surprised by their public display of affection, but in her heart, she was proud to watch them show their love for each other. When her mom finally walked down the hall, her father looked at Maggie sheepishly and shrugged.

"Mom's very lucky to have you, Dad." Then she added, "and so am I," in a very soft voice.

Her dad walked to the freezer and pulled out a pinwheel cookie. He placed one on a paper towel and sat it in front of Maggie. "I'm sorry that I hurt you, sweet pea. I would do anything to make that up to you. I should have told you everything from the very beginning. I had been friends with James for as long as I could remember. I thought he was just blowing off steam and was shocked when I found out otherwise. I'm sorry."

Maggie nodded in acknowledgment, held out her pinwheel cookie, and they tapped them together. "Cheers," they said in unison and bit into the frozen chocolate shell of the cookies.

"I love you, Dad," Maggie said affectionately.

"I love you more." They ate happily while her dad asked her, "Are you getting Lazaretto River Sports ready for business? You'll be re-opening soon."

"Yes, I met with Mac yesterday to go over everything. Our calendar is already booked up, too. That's always a good sign for a great season ahead." She thought about what to say, then tentatively began the conversation. "Hey, what do you know about the land where LRS sits?"

"What do you mean?"

"Well, is there anything strange about it? Or did anything happen there?"

"What's wrong?"

"Nothing. It's just...well, I think it might be haunted."

Her dad looked down at the table, deep in thought, then his eyes met hers. "I've heard stories. Stories from the mouths of children. They always sounded like nonsense to me. When James and I were boys, we would sometimes go to the old fish camp that was at that location with his dad. James told me that the land had been passed down in his family for centuries. It had once been a place to quarantine anyone who carried disease coming to Savannah by ship. He said the people haunted his family, but he didn't know why. I never saw it like that. It was a great piece of property that sat on Lazaretto Creek, and we would fish and swim and have a big time." He looked to Maggie, who was listening intently. "Has something happened?"

"Happened? No. But I hear things. Moans, really. And sometimes, if I'm there late at night, I see movement down on the dock and at the marsh's edge. Kathleen said that the property was majorly haunted. But, over the past two years, nothing bad has happened. Nothing at all. In fact, I almost feel like they are protecting me somehow, but I don't know why. Is that crazy?"

"Nothing is crazy when it comes to ghosts. Will you let me know if you need me for anything?"

"Absolutely, Dad."

"Are you gonna be okay here while we travel?"

Maggie glanced down at all the brochures on the table and thumbed through them. "I'm a big girl now," she said as she slid the sombrero off her head and sat it in the chair beside her. "I've taken care of myself for many years. I'll be fine." Then she looked down at the brochures again and noticed the second one was about Venice. She pulled it out to get a better view and gazed at the photo of the gondolier on the front. Her heart ached as she thought about the night she rode in Leo's gondola. She looked back at her father and said, "The only problem is that I might not be here when you return." She slid the brochure over to her dad. "Do you think you can come to see me in Italy?

34

ALUMNAE

Maggie parked illegally along Lafayette Square and ran up the granite steps of the Cathedral of Saint John the Baptist. She was late for the alumnae Mass, one of the many alumni events that St. Vincent's Academy provided for their past graduates. The massive double doors in the center were locked, meaning that Mass had begun. Maggie grunted and slinked to the smaller door off to the right — the tardy door. As she stepped inside, she was met by the downward stare of one of her favorite nuns, Sister Mary Michael. Maggie cringed and waited to be scolded. No matter how old you are, a nun could still give you a proper scolding. But, instead, the good sister said, "Punctuality is a virtue for the bored." She winked at Maggie, hugged her neck, and motioned to where the tribe was sitting inside the large cathedral.

All her friends glanced over at Maggie as she entered the pew. She shook her head and held up the speeding ticket she had received on the Islands Expressway. They all smiled while Maggie rolled her eyes. Jan had been sitting on the end, and she put her arm around Maggie, whispering in her ear, "We've got to do something about that lead foot of yours."

Saint Vincent's alumni were strong in numbers, but even more powerful in spunk. The school had been graduating fierce young women since 1845 and instilling the values of family, friends, education, and traditions. Not many high schools, or colleges, could fill a cathedral with the number of alumnae that their school did. Maggie looked around and recognized most of the faces in the crowd. The class of 81' had the most graduates present. She smiled, thinking it seemed natural to refer to people by the year they graduated and wondered if that was a Savannah thing.

It was easy to distinguish the difference in the graduating years. The newer graduates were all wearing their cute sundresses and high heels. They huddled close and talked through Mass. The middle-aged graduates were fanning themselves with their programs to combat the hot flashes that each was fighting. And the older graduates sat in the very front. They stood apart by the white hair they no longer tried to cover up. Their love of SVA, and their Catholic faith, inspired Maggie to try harder. She pondered both her speeding ticket and illegal parking job and realized she had a long way to go.

Maggie stifled the cry in the back of her throat when they belted out the Alma Mater at the end of Mass. How could she ever leave Savannah? A tear slid down her cheek, and she brushed it away but not quickly enough. Jan smiled and patted her hand.

The crowd walked over to the gym for lunch. Several of

the alumnae classes would spend their day arguing about who made the best chicken salad for the luncheon. However, this year's argument was who made the worst.

The school had placed a bar directly inside the entrance that served the finest boxed wines ever made. There was a center table set up for all chicken salad contestants. Small plastic containers held a tablespoon-sized scoop of each salad with the lid stating what class it belonged to. Each table held a platter with various types of bread, several kinds of crackers, and scorecards were set at each place. Once everyone had their plates fixed, the tasting began, and so did the chatter.

The wine always loosened their tongues, so the ladies began to jabber before turning in their scorecards. One of the entries tasted sour, so the ladies assumed that the mayonnaise was rancid and asked if it had been left in the car during Mass. Each person whispered to their friends, asking them not to eat it because it would make them sick. The whispering ran rampant through the gym.

The sound of a metal chair scraping the gym floor drew everyone's attention to Maureen Darby. She stood so quickly that her chair toppled. All eyes watched as she stomped to the center table, slid the containers into her enormous tote, and walked out the door with tiny containers spilling out of her purse. The tribe looked to one another and agreed to never make chicken salad for that event in the future.

After the class of '85 won the competition, a full Southern brunch was served. Each of the girls left feeling overly satisfied. Agnes suggested the tribe go for a short walk. Naturally, they all began to walk down Lincoln, across Liberty, and towards Colonial Cemetery. This was a walk they often took between classes at SVA, not because they were morbid and liked being in a cemetery, but because it sat on six acres of downtown property. The grounds held beautiful oaks as old as the cemetery itself. Graceful branches bowed to the ground showing off the Spanish moss that was along for the ride. The property also had secluded paths away from the busy streets with passing cars. Most people in Savannah weren't frightened of cemeteries. They were part of their past, a past they were proud of, not afraid of.

As they came to the spot where four paths crossed, Jan asked Maggie why she cried during the Alma Mater. Softly Maggie answered, "I think I'm going back to Italy."

"I knew it, Maggie. You're in love. How long are you staying this time?" Agnes asked.

Maggie bit her lip as a tear slid down her cheek. She looked up to answer, but the words got stuck in her throat. Finally, she muttered just one word, "Indefinitely."

"What? When did this happen? How are you going to leave Lazaretto River Sports?" Latrice asked.

"Mac will take it over as part owner."

"How are you going to leave your family?" Stephanie asked.

"They are going to be traveling. I asked my parents to come and see me."

"How are you going to leave us?" Kathleen asked.

The waterworks hit hard, and all six of them were crying before long. Each of them had left Savannah at different times, but no one had ever gone for good. Most of the time in Savannah, people moved home, not away.

They were crying so hard, and each tried to talk through

their cries. They didn't notice the sassy tour guide approach, holding his sign high in the air while leading a group of history-hungry tourists.

Maggie saw the group first. She pretended they were grieving over someone who had just been buried and began talking loud to the tribe, "He was a good, good man. I'm gonna miss him so!" The last burial in Colonial Cemetery was in 1850, so the young man just shook his head and said, "Twits!" Their crying then turned into uncontrollable laughter. Maggie knew she would never forget that moment and wondered if she would ever feel the amount of love from friends as she did that day in the cemetery.

Since she was already downtown, Maggie decided to do a little research into the spirits who haunted her office. The day was so lovely she decided to walk to The Georgia Historical Society building on Whitaker Street. She strolled down Abercorn Street, turned on Gaston Street, and skirted Forsyth Park. The view that cut through its center and straight to the fountain always took her breath away. Savannahians never became numb to the beauty of their city.

She was met by a sweet voice as soon as she walked in the front door of The Georgia Historical Society. "Good afternoon, darlin'. What can I help you with?"

The direct question caught Maggie off-guard. How could she say she was researching the ghost in her building without sounding like a looney bird? She decided to ask for information only. "I wanted to get some information on Lazaretto Creek, please."

The sweet lady looked her over and nodded. "What years are you looking for?"

Maggie shrugged, "Maybe, all of them? I really don't know."

The lady smiled. "Tell you what, dear. Why don't we start from the beginning and see what turns up?" Maggie followed her to the massive, three-story-high open ceiling library room. The lady walked to a computer and typed while scribbling down her findings simultaneously. She looked up at Maggie, "If you can't find what you want here, you won't find it anywhere." She scurried along the various shelves, dropping items into Maggie's hands as they walked. When Maggie's arms were full, she motioned her to one of the long wooden tables and said to let her know if Maggie needed anything further.

Maggie began reading. "The Italian word 'lazaretto' means hospital. It comes from the Hebrew word 'lazar,' or 'leper,' referring to the story in the Bible of Lazarus whom Jesus raised from the dead."

Holy crap! Lazaretto Creek is named for a bible story of a man raised from the dead, she thought to herself as she quickly flipped to the following article. Book after book retold the story of the land and the horror of the people who once lived there. "Hundreds dead," "mass burials," and "yellow fever" were the words that kept catching her attention. The more she read, the more agitated she became. Terror washed over her, and she struggled to get a good breath of air. Looking up from the table, her eyes darted around the room to see if anyone noticed she was in turmoil. She immediately locked eyes with the librarian, who offered a slight smile and made her way back to the table.

"It's quite a story, I know. Can I help you with anything?" the librarian asked.

"Yes!" Maggie croaked. Hearing the desperation in her voice, she tried to steady her nerves and answer calmly. "This is a lot to process. I'm going to need some help with all of this, and I know just the person I can lean on. Can you tell me how to make copies of this information?"

An hour later, Maggie left with a file folder full of copied material. She wasn't sure how much a librarian from The Georgia Historical Society got paid, but she knew it was nowhere near what they were worth.

Her path as she left the museum was in no way as peaceful as when she came. She barely remembered passing the Forsyth Fountain. Now that she knew her property truly was haunted, things would never be the same. The next thing she knew, she was on Kathleen's front porch, desperately knocking at the door.

Jack answered quickly, with a dishtowel thrown over his shoulder. He took one look at Maggie's face and nervously said, "Good gosh, you look like you've seen a ghost."

A cry erupted from her throat; Maggie choked out only two words, "I have."

35

SUBMERGED

Venice, Italy

The rhythmic sound of the paddle making contact with the water calmed Leo's restless thoughts. His lack of sleep was taking a toll on him; the previous night had been the worst. He missed Maggie. Although he had called her every day, it just wasn't the same as being together. He needed her, and that thought alone scared the hell out of him.

He had taken the kayak out early that morning as the sun rose over the canal. He snaked his way through the many canals, paddling hard down Rio de S. Lorenzo. Slowing as he turned into Rio de Greci, he studied the Church of Saint George as he passed. It was lovely in warmer months, with green vines billowing over the encasement towards the canal. Yet, now, those vines were bare. It gave the church an eerie feeling. The clock tower chimed seven consecutive times as he passed. He slowed his kayak when he came up beside San Zaccaria Church and inched his way through the heavy wooden doors which had absorbed gallons of seawater over time. They once provided sanctuary for the many who dwelt inside. They now offered comfort to the many barnacles that clung to them for protection.

Once inside the small chapel beneath the still functioning larger church, he steadily paddled down the center aisle. The sun filtering through the stained glass windows imparted strange reflections on the water. The light made it appear as if something was moving beneath him. He shivered involuntarily, but as his eyes focused on the massive marble altar half-submerged in the front of the church, he dared to continue. He bowed his head as he approached, pondering the many Masses that had been held at this exact spot hundreds of years before.

When he and Maggie kayaked into this chapel, she had been overwhelmed by thoughts of stepping into the past. He explained that Venice had been sinking half an inch per 100 years but now increased every year due to human activities. With the sea levels rising, it had become a big problem. He was worried the mystical city would completely disappear into the sea one day. That was when she had told him he *must* open his business. "People need to see this, Leo," she had said as she motioned with her paddle around the chapel. "People should be able to see the beauty and history of Venice before it's too late. It's paying tribute to the people who lived here many years before and paving a future for people who will live here in years to come. This company could not only be an adventure, but could educate others to help save Venice."

He recalled the passion and determination in her eyes when she had spoken. It had inspired him to move forward and had given them a shared mission. He once again felt the thrill in his stomach of guiding groups around by the water. He realized every picture in his head had Maggie at his side, whether in Venice or Savannah. He knew what he had to do. He called Sergio the moment he got back to the office and was sitting in front of Mr. Bianco within the hour.

The smell of Mr. Bianco's espresso wafted through the air, and Leo's stomach growled as he watched him bite into his biscotti. "You're turning down my offer, aren't you, Leo?"

Leo stumbled for the correct response. "I am so honored to be considered. My father held both you and this job in the highest regard. But my pride is what is drawing me to this job. I'm sorry to admit that, but it's true. I wanted the prestige that came with the job. My father named me Leo because of the humility taught by Saint Leo. He taught me that humility disarms the power of pride and weakens the devil's hold. Maggie reminds me of that, just by the way she lives. So, with great regret, I must say no, thank you."

Mr. Bianco nodded, "Ah yes, Maggie, your young lady friend from the States. How is she, by the way? Sergio told me about her mother."

Leo was dumbfounded and wondered, not for the first time, how this one man could know so much about so many people. "She is fine, and her mother is doing well. Thank you for asking. She is back in the States."

"Tell me, Leo, what will become of you?"

"I am in the process of opening an adventure company that will show both locals and tourists alike the beauty of our sinking city from the water. Maggie showed me that to preserve Venice, people need to see what harm they are doing to it. The best way to show this is by sitting in the water on a kayak."

Mr. Bianco sat up further in his chair, listening intently. "Bianco Enterprise invests in many preservation projects. Would you consider a silent partner?"

Surprised by his statement, Leo moved his chair a little closer. The two men discussed many possibilities of their collaboration. Leo left, thanking the older man for everything he had done for him and his family. When he extended his hand for a shake, Mr. Bianco pulled him in close and embraced him. Finally, he double patted both of Leo's shoulders. "We will talk again soon," he said in closing, and Sergio appeared out of thin air and escorted Leo to the door.

Leo walked down the front steps leading to the canal and leaned against a concrete post looking into the murky water. So much had changed in his life, and he wanted to share his joy with someone. When he closed his eyes, he pictured Maggie's smile; he knew he must go to her.

36

CARNIVALE

It had been a long ten days of Carnivale and Monica had been to every party possible. People thought being popular was easy, but it was demanding work. Wearing the right clothes and saying the right things came effortlessly. Still, her indiscretions had become a slight addiction that could turn into a problem.

She never felt guilty for enticing and conquering men. If they ever wavered, she could add a drop of this or that to their wine. That always did the trick. Her only problem was their wives, and they had begun to talk. Their talk could push her out of the social circles she deserved to be in, even if what they said was true.

Shrove Tuesday, the last day of Carnivale, had arrived, reducing her opportunities to misbehave. She could behave for a while and take a break from all the drinking and delicious food. Those extra three pounds in her skin-tight dresses were bothersome. She knew she must attend to them before they became an unwelcome addition to her hourglass figure.

The good Catholics would assume she was making a sacrifice for Lent by fasting and not drinking, but she needed those forty days to let things blow over a bit. Everybody knew that Carnivale was just a prelude for the upcoming summer, and that was when the serious fun began.

Shrove Tuesday had been packed full of events such as parading the streets in period costumes and the Flight of the Angel from Saint Mark's bell tower. She still had the Biancos' dinner honoring her husband and then the final Carnivale ball. Although she could hardly wait for the evening, she dreaded the dinner with every fiber of her being. Pietro had been so excited, pulling out his tuxedo from the closet and brushing off the dust covered shoulders from the year before. He had requested she buy him a new bow tie, but she had pushed aside his request. He was so needy, and it aggravated her. She was exhausted from the long week. If only she could take a nap before the big ball. Surely, they wouldn't notice her absence at the dinner. She smiled at the thought of her crisp sheets on her bed and made her way home.

Pietro stood with Michael outside of the Biancos' home. He had asked Mr. Bianco to wait five more minutes before giving his speech. Walking out the front door that overlooked the Grand Canal, he worriedly called Monica one last time. Surely, something had happened to her; she never would have missed this dinner. She knew how much it meant to him. When Mr. Bianco asked him inside, he knew he couldn't hold him off any longer. The dinner had been excellent, and Mr. Bianco's speech had been very heartfelt, but he still worried about Monica. The dinner guest who sat nearby glanced at the empty chair, offering him a sad nod. However, he kept hoping Monica would show up and wouldn't let the staff clear her chair. Over dessert, Michael had whispered how proud he was of him, which made everything he did worthwhile.

Mr. Bianco watched Pietro through dinner. It was obvious to see his and Michael's love for one another. They talked and cut up through the seven-course meal. Pietro held his head high, even though his wife had been a no-show. Unfortunately, Monica had not been a no-show at all of the other parties around Venice for the last ten days. The person who had been tailing her had given Mr. Bianco a full report earlier that morning. But that report wasn't the only one that had found its way onto Mr. Bianco's desk. A manila envelope had been left with a ledger of all the people Monica had been meeting with. It held many names Mr. Bianco knew well, including some known to be ruthless in business and pleasure. Whoever had left that ledger had been watching Monica for years and years. Mr. Bianco made a copy of its contents and placed it back into the envelope.

Mr. Bianco felt Sergio's eyes on him; Sergio motioned toward Monica's open seat. Mr. Bianco nodded, knowing it was time to tell Pietro the whole story, and had Sergio ask him and Michael for a nightcap after dinner.

Once the three men were seated, Mr. Bianco offered the men grappa poured into tulip-shaped glasses. After Pietro had emptied his glass, Mr. Bianco told him of Monica's betrayal and how Michael had followed her direction. Pietro looked to Michael, who only nodded in agreement. Mr. Bianco then handed Pietro both the envelope with a full report on his wife over the last month and the ledger. He was impressed at Pietro's strength and was surprised when he stood up, thanked him, and started for the door.

Mr. Bianco extended his hand, "I am honored to have you as my gondolier. You are a true friend."

Pietro shook his boss's hand, "It's my honor, sir. I will be here first thing in the morning to escort you to Ash Wednesday Mass at Saint Mark's. Good evening."

Michael broke as soon as they were on the sidewalk, "I'm sorry, Papa. I never meant to hurt anyone. I can't believe I was so weak that I listened to Mom. It hurt so many people. Will you ever forgive me?"

Pietro hugged his son, then kissed him on both cheeks, "I will always forgive you. Will you forgive me?"

"Whatever for?" Michael asked.

Pietro paused for a long time, took a deep breath, and looked Michael in the eye, "For not following my gut. For turning my head to so many things. But most of all, for not seeing the hurt in your eyes all year long."

A tear slowly fell down Michael's cheek, "I really thought I would feel relieved after you knew the truth, but something is still hanging over my head."

"Maybe there is someone else you need to apologize to. Claudio's family may not accept it, and I wouldn't blame them if they didn't. Still, until you apologize, this will continue to be hanging over your head." Michael nodded in agreement. "Want to ride out to Sant' Erasmus tomorrow afternoon?"

The two of them stood on Ponte Santa Margherita, the bridge closest to their house, and watched the fireworks coming from the Grand Ball. When Pietro and Michael finally walked into their empty home, Pietro went straight to his bedroom. He hung up the tuxedo and the old bowtie and placed them back in the closet until next year. He then looked around his room at the many expensive dresses lying about. He always believed he was the lucky one to have married Monica. He knew she wasn't perfect, but he was grateful for whatever time and attention she gave him. But this time, she had gone too far.

He sat at the end of the bed, opened the envelope Mr. Bianco had given him, and glanced at its contents. Bile rose to the back of his throat, so he stood quickly until the feeling passed. He tossed the envelope in the bedside table drawer and climbed into the bed where, more times than not, he slept in alone. His heart hurt, but now he knew, and once he knew, he couldn't go back.

37

BLESSING OF THE FLEET

Tybee Island, Georgia

The driver moved at a snail's pace down Tybee Road. As the car crept over the last bridge onto the island, Leo started noticing the vehicles lining the street, but he was too focused on surprising Maggie to be interested.

He had practiced his speech repeatedly on the plane and could barely contain his excitement. He asked the driver to take him by Lazaretto River Sports on the way to Maggie's house. When he saw her jeep at the office, he threw his luggage in the parking lot and ran in the front door. He called out her name, but the office was empty. The only sounds he heard were coming from the workshop in the back of the building, so he followed.

Old rock-'n'-roll music blasted while Mac worked. Only when Leo was standing in front of his workbench did Mac finally notice him. As the older man looked up, a smile spread across his face. Leo felt the friendship the two men had for one another. Mac tossed down the pliers he was holding and pulled Leo in for an emotional hug, then laughed awkwardly as he let him go. "Thank God above! Maggie has been moping around for weeks. That girl's got it bad."

"Where is she? I really need to talk to her."

"You just missed her. The first Saturday in March is always the Blessing of the Fleet on Tybee. She just rowed off to get into line." Then he paused, contemplating what he was about to say. "Wanna join her?" He walked to the back of the workspace and pulled a large tarp off a boat.

"Mac, you shouldn't have." Leo rubbed his hand down the side, admiring the man's handiwork. Then with a grin, he said, "But I'm damn glad you did."

MAGGIE WAS FIGHTING the water's natural tendency to run out of the creek; she struggled to keep her kayak in the line of boats. They had placed her last where she wouldn't hold up all the motorized watercraft. The larger vessels had either pulled alongside docks or anchored to keep their position. Maggie's small kayak was constantly moving. The boat parade was scheduled to shove off at 9:45 a.m. and pass under the Lazaretto Creek Bridge at 10:00 for the blessing. Everything was running thirty minutes late, as usual for Tybee time.

Maggie was tiring quickly, so she paddled away from the group and found a spot to pull onto the mud embankment of the marsh. Her arms already ached, and the parade hadn't even begun. She looked over at all the boats participating this year: shrimp boats, deep-sea fishing boats, dolphin tours, jet ski rental boats, several personal small-craft boats, and her kayak. Within each group, people laughed and enjoyed the warm morning, some with drinks already in hand. She suddenly felt alone and now wished she had taken Mac up on his offer to come along.

Once the mayor made his way to the starting point, she furiously paddled back to her place at the rear of the group. She was so focused on staying in line and in the view of the larger boats that she didn't feel the other kayak move in beside her.

"*Ciao, bella!* Oh, how I've missed you!" Maggie almost fell out of her boat as she turned to meet the voice. There he sat, Leo, in a black gondola-like kayak.

"Leo, you're here!" she screamed as butterflies fluttered in her stomach. Their kayaks bumped as they both reached to grab the other's boat to pull close to one another. He leaned towards her but struggled while trying to hold his paddle. They both laughed when he awkwardly planted a wet kiss on her face. At that moment, all doubt left her. She never wanted to be apart from him again...no matter what.

Leo laughed, "Well, this isn't how I pictured our reunion when I was on the plane, but I'm overjoyed to see your sweet face."

Maggie motioned Leo to their place in line as the boats began to make way. Once they were moving, she was able to inspect his gondola-kayak. "Is that my old fishing kayak?"

"Yes, with several adjustments."

"And when did you do this?"

"Mac and I worked on it last fall. He finished it while we were in Italy. He said he had a feeling I would return."

The men had taken the large kayak and added a double hull and a small platform on the back where the trolling motor once sat. Then they framed the bow and the stern, using chicken wire and black marine vinyl, and flipped up the front and back. Finally, they painted everything black so that it actually appeared to be a gondola.

"Have you tried standing and rowing yet?"

"Are you kidding me? This boat weighs a ton. Mac wasn't even sure if this thing would float. He wished me good luck when he pushed me from the dock and started whistling the tune to *Gilligan's Island* as he walked off."

Maggie was in a full laugh as they paddled their way out of the creek, struggling to keep up with the speed of the motorized vessels but falling way behind. However, as they brought up the rear of the line of boats going under the bridge, their kayaks were blessed just the same. She chuckled, saying, "The first will be last, and the last will be first."

The parade continued to pass by the many onlookers standing along the beach. Everyone cheered as they waved on their fleet of boats for the year ahead. Maggie paddled as far as she could, then she and Leo turned away from the group and rode the tide back towards the dock.

"I'm thrilled you're here," Maggie told Leo. Her stomach rolled with excitement at the sight of him.

"We have much to discuss," he said.

Maggie agreed but was interrupted by a family of dolphins who surfaced between them while chasing fish down the creek. They stopped paddling and watched the dolphins surround the fish and push them up on the mud.

One by one, each dolphin banked itself in the mud and enjoyed the fish that it had chased on the bank for a meal. Leo had never seen this before, and it worried him. "Why would a fish ever bank itself on purpose?"

"There is nowhere else in the world where dolphin hunt this way. Only in the Low Country. Marine biologists have no explanation. It only happens in pods, and they always slide their way back into the river," Maggie explained.

Leo watched in awe but secretly could relate. He had acted on instinct in coming to Savannah but was willing to sacrifice everything for Maggie. He sat open and exposed, just like these dolphins. He prayed Maggie would be by his side to make sure he stayed afloat.

When they returned to the office, Mac sat in front of the television watching the news at noon. The camera showed the priest standing on top of the Lazaretto Bridge, sprinkling holy water, followed by the procession of boats. The reporter explained that all boats were blessed the first week in March, even though the shrimp season didn't begin for a few months.

The tanned reporter popped back on camera when the report seemed to be over. In her heavy southern drawl, she announced, "This yearly tradition had a new twist this year. Is that a gondola coming down our creek? I can't wait to find out." Then the camera zoomed in on Leo and Maggie. Leo had steadied himself to stand on the back platform of the kayak. Since Maggie had been sitting down in her kayak next to him, she didn't realize how Leo's boat looked from the shore, but it looked exactly like a gondola. Then the camera continued to zoom in on the two of them for all of the world to see. Their smiles beamed at each other. Maggie was embarrassed as she watched but couldn't avert her eyes from the TV screen. If she had any doubt whatsoever before, it was now confirmed. The camera didn't lie; they were in love.

The news show continued and moved on to the weather forecast, but Maggie and Leo sat glued to the television. Finally, Mac cleared his throat and brought them back to the present. "Okay, you love birds; I'm heading out. I'll see you tonight at the Fleet Party."

Excited that she and Leo were alone, Maggie began to bite her lower lip. Leo immediately picked up on her feelings and ran his hand down the side of her face, then rubbed the bite mark that remained on her lip. "You'll never know how much I've missed you, Maggie. Nothing is the same without you."

"I know exactly how you feel. All my life, I've been happy living in Savannah, but now nothing makes sense without you." Maggie took a deep breath, trying to swallow the lump in her throat. Leo's hand remained on the side of her face, then slowly moved to the back of her neck and pulled her in close. As their lips connected, a small moan escaped from him as if he was surrendering everything to her.

He pulled back, shaking his head, "I can't go on without you."

She placed her hand over his and said in a whisper, "Then let's go on together."

38

BEACH MUSIC

T he sounds of beach music traveled through the air as Leo and Maggie walked along Main Street toward the Fleet Party. Strands of lights hung, illuminating the street like a landing strip all the way to the pavilion. Children ran across the park with water guns, each trying to see how long their liquid ammunition could last before stopping to refill.

When Maggie stopped at the first booth to purchase a beer, the owner yelled out, "It's on the house for our celebrity gondolier." Leo had no idea at the time, but the eyes of the partygoers would be on him all night long. They walked down the pier then further onto the pavilion. The structure was built over the water, allowing beachgoers and boaters to enjoy the facility.

Maggie looked for her friends who came to the party every year. As they approached the stage, the band began to play, "That's Amore," and everybody turned to stare. The main singer excitedly announced, "New to the fleet this year, let's give a good ole Southern welcome to our Savannah Gondolier." The crowd erupted in applause. Leo waved while Maggie scanned the room, looking for her friends. She smiled as she located the group, standing around a high-top table just off the dance floor. The promise of a fun-filled evening, shared with her best friends and the man she loved, filled Maggie with excitement and contentment.

As Leo gave a wildly exaggerated bow, the band began their next song, "I Love Beach Music." Maggie motioned to her friends to join them on the dance floor. Leo offered his hand to Maggie for a dance but then hesitated after noticing everyone was doing a dance unfamiliar to him called the Shag. He asked her to explain the steps to him as he swayed back and forth. Maggie smiled at the thought of her dad teaching her the Shag at the Fleet Party when she was a little girl and pictured her bare feet standing on his flip-flops while learning the steps. "It goes one and two, three and four, five-six." Then showing him, she said, "Step, step, step; step step step; back step," repeatedly until he began to follow along.

Kathleen and Jack, followed by Jan and Eddie, shuffled up next to them and fell right in step. Both Kathleen and Jan were so excited to see Leo they welcomed him with a hug. Then Jack grabbed Kathleen's hand and pulled her into a spin. "Come on, hot mama, show me your moves," he said to his wife.

Kathleen winked at Maggie then turned her full attention back to Jack. "Oh, you can't handle *my* moves, old man." They all laughed as Jack expertly spun Kathleen around like he had done hundreds of times in their marriage. Leo watched how Jack anticipated Kathleen's every move as he spun her around like a pro. This made Leo refocus his attention.

By the end of the song, Leo was shagging much better, but he never stopped counting out loud. When the band took a break, the dancers grabbed the rest of the group from the table and walked to the beer booth to consume more liquid courage before returning to the dance floor. They wandered onto the beach, threw their shoes off, and settled directly underneath the dance floor. The cold from the sand, which only hours before had been scorching hot, ran its coolness up Maggie's legs as she crunched the grains between her toes.

Maggie dug her big toe down a little deeper in the sand, like a ghost crab seeking coverage, and swayed to the music above. Since the others were talking to one another, she was the first to hear the lone guitar play the simple notes, and she screamed, "Oh, my gosh! This is our song! Get your asses up!" They all quieted to listen. Once they realized it was "Under the Boardwalk," they began to dance, balancing their red Solo cups in one hand while holding their partner's hand in the other. When the chorus started, they all joined in, dancing on the sand until the band finished for the night.

The following morning, Maggie woke to the smell of coffee and a note scribbled on a paper towel: *Caffè and come all' acqua.*

Smiling, she pondered how Leo spoke English so well but couldn't write it. She poured a mug of coffee and walked toward the dock. Her cat, Joe, watched as she crossed the dew-covered lawn in her terry-cloth slippers, but he quickly went back to chasing a cricket near the garden.

Leo had carried the Adirondack chairs to her floating dock and was watching the colors of the sky. The sunrises were one of the many perks of living on the backside of Tybee. He didn't hear her approach, so she slowed, watching his face and pondering what his thoughts might be. She wondered how close she could get to him before he felt her presence. Leo turned at her very next step, and the look on his face told it all. He loved her. She would never forget that moment.

She sat in the chair beside his and finally took the first sip of coffee. Sighing, she said, "The first sip is always the best. Thank you for brewing it." She stole a glance at Leo over her mug, then set the cup on the giant arm of the chair.

Leo turned and took her hand. "The water drew us together as kids and brought us back together as adults, so it seemed fitting to ask you this on the water."

Ask me this? Oh, my gosh. Is he proposing to me? Can this really be happening? Maggie thought as she gave her full attention to him. "When you left Venice, nothing was the same. I realized you are a part of every plan I have made for the future and every decision that I will make. I'm not sure what our life together will look like at this point, but I know that I want you; No, I need you at my side." He got out of his chair, kneeled in front of her, and pulled out a ring. "Maggie, will you marry me?"

Maggie screamed, "Yes!" and sprung from her chair. She forgot that she was sitting in the Adirondack, and the angle of its seat threw off her balance. Her coffee cup went flying as she fell onto the dock right in front of Leo. "Are you all right?" he asked while pulling her to her feet.

She was so excited; she felt no pain. "I'm better than all right. I'm wonderful."

He took her in his arms and kissed her, "Yes, you are. You're wonderful. And you're going to be my wife."

She began to jump up and down, and it shook the dock. "We're getting married," she said through her laughter, but as the concept began to sink in, she stopped bouncing and started asking questions. "Where are we going to live? Where are we having the wedding? Did you ask my dad for permission?"

He looked down at her coffee-covered clothes and smiled, "Yes, I asked your dad, and funny enough, he had the same questions. Let's go to the house and let you change out of your wet shirt. We have much to discuss." Leo scooped her in his arms, just as he had done in front of her friends in Forsyth Park. This time, he didn't set her down. He carried her across the wet lawn and inside the small cottage, then he gave her a proper kiss. Things had changed entirely in a matter of minutes, and she could feel the electricity in the air.

The next kiss held the promise of forever. A tingle ran down Maggie's spine as she melted into him. Maggie nibbled his ear. "Did you say we had things to discuss?" she teased.

"All discussions can wait," Leo said in a whisper, and he covered her mouth with his.

39

SAVANNAH'S SAINT PATRICK'S DAY

T ybee felt like perpetual summer, summoning its residents outside to enjoy the warmth of the sun. Maggie and Leo jumped on bikes and rode towards Butler Avenue. She had the perfect view of her new engagement ring with her hand on the handlebars. Her stomach clenched with excitement as the sunlight set the solitaire diamond afire.

"I'm glad we decided to wait to tell everyone until later today. We still need to talk. This fresh air should help clear our minds," Leo said.

Maggie felt a pang of guilt for calling Kathleen while Leo was in the shower, but how many times does a girl get engaged? She couldn't hold in her excitement any longer without bursting. She peddled, counting off the many numbered streets leading down to the Atlantic Ocean. Once they hit 7th Street, they turned towards the beach.

They walked across a long wooden walkway that ran over the dunes and were lucky to find an empty wooden bench swing at the end, just waiting for them. Maggie hopped up into the swing, letting her legs dangle while Leo kept a steady pace. The smell of the fresh coastal breeze always balanced her, and she needed that balance right now. They had important decisions to make about their future. She spun her ring, taking a deep breath, as she contemplated the many unknowns of her future.

Deep in thought, Leo quietly watched as she fiddled with her new ring. The time had come, so he started the conversation they needed to have; the sooner, the better.

"Will you come to Venice?" he blurted out. "We could come back to Savannah before summer begins. Venice Kayak Tours is up and running now. So much has happened; I want to fill you in." Maggie forced herself to focus on Leo's words, not the anxiety building inside her.

"Mr. Bianco agreed with everything you said about people needing to see Venice first-hand so they can assist in preserving the city's history. He was very interested in our kayak business and offered to be a silent partner. He is trying to find a second location on the other side of Venice. Davide is now a full-time employee and the second in command. Correction, third in command once we are married. Davide is a natural on the water and has a great business sense. He did a great job hiring and training our instructors. Opening day is April 1st, but we could push it back if we need to. What do you think?"

Maggie's shoulders tensed. "You've been busy in my absence," she replied. She couldn't quite put her finger on what she was feeling, but it felt pretty close to fear. Maggie knew she and Leo were meant to be together, but she was worried. Leo studied her reaction, waiting for an answer.

"I think that's wonderful," she said with more enthusiasm than she actually felt. "I can leave any time after St. Patrick's Day. Lazaretto River Sports has a float registered for the parade. You don't mind, do you?"

Leo looked surprised, "No, but only if you let me ride on it."

"Deal," she said, thinking how sweet it was that Leo wanted to be in the parade. She suddenly had a unique idea for the float. She couldn't wait to speak with Mac to see if he could help her create this year's entry in the two short weeks before the festivities.

Maggie spent that afternoon sharing the news of her engagement with her friends and reassuring them that she wasn't moving to Italy, at least not for now. She and Leo had purchased plane tickets departing the week after St. Patrick's Day and had purchased return flights to be back in Savannah before summer. She had a busy few weeks before they left.

MAC AND MAGGIE worked on the float for days. They borrowed a flatbed trailer and decorated its bed to look like water. Then they mounted the boat in its center. Next, they attached a rail on the back of the gondola-kayak for Leo to secure himself during the parade. When they finally let Leo see the finished product, he was excited and impressed.

The fake gondola appeared to float down the two-and-a-half-mile parade route. Maggie walked beside Leo, throwing candy and beads into the crowd, while Mack pulled the trailer with his pick-up truck. Maggie had also rented a speaker and was blasting Italian music.

As they approached Lafayette Square, Maggie started looking for her friends. Every year, Jack and his buddies held the same spot in the square, and it didn't come easily. The city of Savannah had many rules to accommodate the number of people attending. They began barricading the walkways the day before. Still, they never allowed anyone to mark off their personal areas in the squares until the event day. Over time, the tricky Irishmen of Savannah interpreted the "day of" to mean 12:01 a.m. Many Irish families stood on the edge of the squares waiting for the clock to hit midnight, then there would be a mad rush for a coveted spot along the parade route. There were fights as the men set up their tents and spread out their chairs in the dark, but everyone made peace before daylight and enjoyed the celebration.

As the Lazaretto River Sports float approached, Maggie heard Kathleen's familiar ear-piercing whistle. Kathleen used her index and middle finger of both hands and blew with just the proper force to be heard up to a mile away. Her dad had taught her the trick when Kathleen was a little girl. Such a whistle was precisely what a mom of five rambunctious kids needed to keep them all in line.

Near Kathleen, a group of people emerged from under the tent, walking towards the street and cheering. Jack broke through the crowd and ran towards the float, handing Leo a Perroni in a plastic cup. Leo yelled down, "You really are a great friend. I'll get the next round." As the parade continued to move towards the cathedral, they waived one last time to their friends. They all knew to meet afterward for the party at the Knights of Columbus hall.

Most of the people cheering for the float were female. Glancing at Leo, she understood why. He was fit, with large muscled arms and a trim waistline from years of rowing. He waved with such enthusiasm, flashing his million-dollar smile. The women responded to his waves, calling out to try to get his attention, while he was oblivious to the comments they were screaming at him. He just kept waving. How did she get so lucky?

The parade wound its way around the many squares and streets of downtown Savannah. At the end of the route, the LRS float passed the judging table. Maggie told Leo to give his best gondolier impression. Leo put on a show like he was steering an authentic gondola in the water. As he looked up to the judges, he noticed a row of young boys sitting in front of the table, and the smallest one stuck out his tongue. Leo began to belly laugh and turned to Maggie, saying, "Just when you think you're on the top of the world, it only takes one person sticking their tongue out at you to bring you back to reality." They laughed and threw the last of their candy at the boys.

After the parade, Leo and Maggie met up with the tribe. Everyone wore their best kelly-green outfits, the ones only worn in March. They were put away on March 18th for the following St. Patrick's Day season, which ran for several weeks before the parade. Hundreds of people were packed into the ballroom, sloshing green beer and leaving lipstick kisses on each other's faces.

When Maggie spotted her friends across the room, she made a bee-line to them. Pulling them in close, she shared the news that Leo wanted to stay in Savannah. Suddenly, her friends stopped listening. Something else captured their attention: Trevor. His eyes left Maggie's face quickly and scanned down to her hand. "So, it's true?" He held her gaze, waiting for an answer.

She nodded, "I finally met someone who puts me above everything else in his world."

Trevor acknowledged her comment and nodded in agreement. "I thought I would be nothing without my dream job, but now I realize I am nothing without you. I made the wrong choice, and I'm sorry."

She let his words sink in, trying to pinpoint what she was feeling. Was it closure? She had given her heart entirely to Leo. There was no room for anyone else. There were no tugs on her heart. It was just water under the bridge that she allowed to be carried away with the outgoing tide.

Leo sidled up to Maggie's side and quizzically looked from one to the other. Trevor extended his hand to Leo, saying, "Congratulations." Turning to Maggie, Trevor leaned over and gently kissed her on the cheek, whispering, "I hope you two are happy. Truly, I do, Mags." Then he disappeared into the crowd.

The tribe had witnessed the whole scene. "They're not serving popcorn with this show, so y'all can stop watching," Maggie teased. Although they all laughed, she continued to feel their eyes on her. That's what they did: watched out for one another.

40

LAZARETTO CREEK

After uncovering the information on Lazaretto Creek the week prior, Maggie and Kathleen had called in the troops for help. Maggie's friends showed up at her office with a sleeping bag and their designated overnight "essential."

"I brought dinner," Agnes announced and plopped down three large pizzas from Huc-A-Poo's and a bottle of wine.

Kathleen motioned Agnes to set the pizza on the table beside her homemade peach cobbler and banana pudding. Kathleen had also brought a bottle of wine.

Stephanie walked in behind Agnes. "I brought the entertainment: cards, Bananagrams, the old Dating Game board game, flashlights...just in case, and a bottle of vino."

Jan plopped down the video equipment she had borrowed from a fellow teacher at SCAD. "It took me forever to learn to use this, but I'll be ready to record any unwanted guests if they surface." Then she reached into the case and added another bottle of wine to the table.

Latrice was the last person in. She walked to the table and looked at the five bottles of wine and then at the group. "Hold on a minute. I was told to bring the alcohol, so I brought Champagne and OJ for mimosas. I think we might have a problem here, ladies." They all looked at her curiously until she added, "Do we have enough?"

Laughing, everyone set up their sleeping bags for the night and then pulled up around the table. Once everyone was eating, Maggie explained the situation. "So, turns out, this land belonged to Trevor's family. It's been passed down for many generations with one stipulation; it could never be sold. His dad didn't want the land, so he got rid of it when he inherited it.

"I thought you said it could never be sold," Jan interrupted.

"Yes, he outsmarted the stipulation and bet it away in a poker game. My dad was the lucky winner, and he gave it to me."

"Wait," Stephanie said, shaking her head. "Your business is on your ex-boyfriend's land? That's pretty messed up."

"Girl, don't I know it," Maggie answered. "Okay, you now understand the present; let me explain the past. The government leased this land from Trevor's great, great, hell, let's just say many times great uncle in the mid-1700s. It was a remote tract of land on the outskirts of Savannah. Early on, our seaport city realized that if diseases like yellow fever or cholera were brought into the city, it would be devastating." Maggie pointed to the ground, "All incoming ships were first stopped here. The sick were forced to remain in a building here until they were cured or," Maggie cleared her throat, "or until they passed."

Stephanie quickly rose to her feet, "Didn't most people die from yellow fever?"

Maggie answered, "Yes, they did."

Stephanie's eyes darted around, "Oh Lord, I don't like where this is going."

"I know. I don't either. But here we are. Let me finish, okay?" Stephanie nodded, and Maggie continued. "Lazaretto, in Italian, means hospital. I didn't know that until Leo told me, and I had no idea it directly affected me. Anyway, by the late 1700s, it held European immigrants who contracted contagious diseases on their transatlantic voyages. It also served as the 'welcoming station' for a host of enslaved Africans after their horrendous passage. Some welcoming, right? People were also brought here throughout the Revolution. To my best estimation, hundreds of people died here and were buried nearby in unmarked graves."

"I'm out," Stephanie said and started gathering her things.

Kathleen rose and put her arm around Stephanie. "I knew this place was haunted when we came to Maggie's open house. But it's not like these are ghosts that move things around and are out for revenge. It's more like a movie clip of the past. I heard their voices, but they weren't speaking to me directly. Maggie just wants to be sure everything is what it seems before she leaves town."

Latrice jumped in, "Just so we are all on the same page, this place *is* haunted, right?"

"Yes," Maggie and Kathleen said in unison.

"All right, then. Let's get this fright-night started." Latrice turned on some music and started mixing the mimosas. Stephanie slowly nodded and sat back down.

Before long, they were all sipping and talking as they always did, and by the time they finished the third bottle of wine, they had come up with a plan for the night. They would each take an hour look-out post while the others slept. They drew names out of a hat, and each knew her schedule. But schedules fly out the window when women and wine are mixed. By two in the morning, six snoring women were laid out on the floor with arms strewn over each other's faces.

They woke to the sound of gunfire. Each of them stumbled into consciousness, searching for the source of the boom. The full moon lent Maggie the ability to see the movement on the dock. She picked up the emergency flare gun by the back door and ran out. Jan had grabbed the video equipment and was recording. She ran out after Maggie, with the rest of the group following.

Halfway down the dock, Maggie had stopped, and they all ran into each other. Maggie pointed as everyone watched in dismay. There were shadows of people walking back and forth across the dock. Dark figures without faces. Men, women, and older children. Some stumbled while others tried to help them back on their feet. They continued to walk past where the dock ended, suspended in air but on a path they once walked until eventually, they disappeared.

Another gunshot brought their eyes from the ghostly spirits and down to the water. Two small boats were racing away. The men inside the boats had seen the spirits and were trying to escape. But they weren't the only ones trying to escape. Stephanie was hysterical, swinging her arms and trying to get to safety. Unfortunately, she was the clumsiest of the group, so when she turned to run back to the house, her feet got caught in a cast net sitting on the dock, and she stumbled and fell.

"*Man down, man down!*" Agnes yelled as they pulled their eyes from the ghosts to Stephanie. They all crouched on the dock, struggling to free Stephanie from the net, when another shot was fired. This time, Maggie heard it fly over their heads and lodge itself into a nearby piling, splintering the wood with a deafening sound. As Maggie spun, she noticed two of her kayaks floating up in the marsh and realized these men were trying to steal her boats. They didn't even see the tribe on the dock. That bullet could have hit any of them.

Maggie stood up, raised the flare gun, and fired it into the air. The tribe all froze and watched the flare climb into the sky. The bright light made the spirits vanish as the men in the boats disappeared down the creek. When the Coast Guard rounded the corner, Maggie pointed down the creek. She yelled above their idling engines, "Two boats just tried to steal from my dock and opened fire towards the house." The Coast Guard wasted no time with further questions and made way in pursuit of the men.

THE FOLLOWING DAY, the ladies were awakened by a knock on the creek-side door. Maggie rubbed her eyes as she opened it to the Coast Guardsmen.

"Thanks to you, we apprehended two stolen boats and the three men who had shot at you. They made-up some story about ghosts but didn't deny that they were trying to steal all of your kayaks and your Scout boat."

Maggie laughed, "Ghosts? Please. They are hoodlums, that's all."

"Don't we know it, ma'am?" They looked around the room at the scattered sleeping bags and empty wine bottles, then grinned. "We'll let you get back to it. Good day!"

As Maggie shut the door, the ladies all giggled.

"Hoodlums, Maggie?" Agnes asked.

"Oh, you're one to talk. *'Man down, Man down.'* Really, Agnes?"

They all were belly laughing as Agnes answered. "I have no idea how that came out. My brothers would always yell that when they made me play army with them when we were little. I guess it stuck."

"We almost were playing army out there," Kathleen added. "We were shot at last night. Any one of us could have been hit with that bullet. Jack would have killed me if I had been killed last night."

"Thank God for my clumsiness," Stephanie chimed in. "Who would have thought I'd ever say that, but it's the truth. If y'all weren't bent over helping me, anything could have happened." Everyone nodded in agreement and thanked Stephanie for being a clutz.

Latrice cleared her throat, "Hey, did you guys notice those Coast Guardsmen? They were checking us out." They looked at one another, all disheveled with their makeup smeared and hair flying in all directions, and laughed.

"Yeah, we are one fine-looking group of gals; we should get a picture together to remember this night," Jan said. As she reached to pick up her camera, she realized the video player was sitting beside it. She began fiddling with it while Maggie got everyone's attention.

"Listen, y'all. We all know what we saw on the dock last night. But, I truly believe that we are meant to protect this land and help to educate others about the people who died here. I'm not sure what that looks like, but we owe it to them."

They all agreed and began to run ideas by one another. They were interrupted by a banging in the front room, followed by a very confused Mac coming through the door.

"Did I miss the party?" he asked.

Maggie spoke up, "Not really a party, per se, but I have some news for you." Mack nodded in acknowledgment. "This place is haunted."

"I know," Mac said. "Is that your news?"

"You know? Why didn't you say anything to me?"

"I thought you knew, too. But they aren't really here. Just a lingering glimpse of the past." He walked past the group, took down a paddle from the back wall, and left.

"So there's that," Jan said. "Leave it to a man to keep things simple. But look what I have," She raised the recorder she had been toying with and began to play the reel. The recording looked like the "Blair Witch Project." The tape was jostled while running down the dock. But when it stilled, it focused on the wandering spirits. The group was silent until Jan asked. "Do you think I should accidentally erase this?"

They all agreed. That would be the first step of many to protect the land.

41

EVERY MAN HAS HIS LIMITS

Venice, Italy

Monica sat at her vanity, carefully applying the red lipstick that perfectly matched her dress. She was both shocked and intrigued to have received a last-minute invitation to the dinner that evening. Typically only forty dinner party invitations were sent for each dinner party to match the forty chairs around the Biancos' formal dining table. She recalled past pictures of the monthly dinners in Venetian society magazines as she ran her finger over the words on Mr. Bianco's personal stationery. It was as if he were begging her to attend. Too bad Pietro would be busy that evening, or was it? Without him holding her back, her options were open. She thought about all she had done to bring herself back into the spotlight and, once again, patted herself on the back. She really was brilliant, and she was so happy that everything was finally working to her advantage.

Mr. Bianco sent one of the many local gondoliers kept on reserve to shuttle Monica to his mansion. As the boat traveled down the canal, she could feel the many bystanders watching. She relished in their jealous stares. How they wished they could be in her shoes.

Once the boat was tied up in front of the house, she was escorted up the candle-lit pebbled walkway and into the Biancos' home. The attendant slipped her wrap off her shoulders and put it away while Sergio welcomed her. That amused her, as she recalled how pompous he once was to her. She nodded but showed him little interest. As she followed him down the grand hallway, he turned into a small alcove. *How divine*, she thought. *Mr. Bianco must be expecting me for a drink.* She briefly toyed with the notion that he might have a sexual interest in her. The thought made her stomach tingle with excitement.

She gracefully entered the sitting room, Sergio pulling the door closed behind her. Mr. Bianco, dressed in a black tuxedo that showed his expensive taste, was standing in front of the large arched window. He was looking out over the darkness of the canal. Even from the back, she saw Mr. Bianco was a man with a strength that stopped her in her tracks. She could dominate a weak man, but a man with power slightly intimidated her.

He turned slightly at the sound of the shutting door, but he continued to stare out into the night. She nervously shifted her weight from one stiletto to the other and willed herself to remain still until he turned again. After what seemed like an eternity, he spun around, and she gasped as she looked into the eyes of a man that she no longer recognized.

He approached her slowly, like an animal on the hunt. Before she could move away, he closed the gap between them, and they stood nose to nose. Fear tightened her throat, and tears burned her eyes, but she was helpless to break his gaze. It penetrated her. She tried to swallow, but her mouth was bone dry. He grabbed her upper arms with great force and pulled her into a deep kiss, exploring her mouth with his tongue as she struggled against his strength.

When he released her, she brought her hand to her now bruised lips as she swallowed the flavor of his scotch that lingered on her tastebuds. He took a step back as she felt the tear slide down her cheek. Looking down into her eyes, he said, "Every man has his limits! Exploiting our son was mine. We are done. Goodbye, Monica," and her husband walked out of the study.

Monica let out a gut-wrenching cry. How had she not recognized Pietro? She ran down the hallway after him, calling his name. He continued, ignoring her pleas, and turned into the dinner party, the same dinner party that she thought she had been invited to. She ran to follow him into the room, but the doors closed in her face. Two men appeared on either side of her and escorted her out the door and onto the street. This time, no gondola was waiting, and she realized that there would never be another gondola waiting – not for someone who was now unimportant.

42

PART OF THE FAMILY

The boat cut its way across the lagoon as Maggie watched the island slowly come into view. The smell of salt-water marsh welcomed her back to San Erasmus. A feeling of warmth overtook her. She had missed the island; she felt like she was coming home.

The entire family came outside when they heard the boat idling down the canal. They walked as a group, with Rosa in the middle, and all talked at the same time. Maggie smiled at the sight and wished she had a picture to memorialize the moment. *This is going to be my family now*, she thought, tears welding in her eyes.

Leo grabbed the luggage as they made their way up the small dock. As Rosa walked towards them, she passed Leo and went straight to Maggie. Pulling Maggie into a long embrace, Rosa whispered in her ear. *"Benvenuti nella nostra famiglia,"* then repeated herself in English, "Welcome to our family." Maggie could not hold back her joyful tears and smiled as she wiped them away. The family encircled her, hugging her and kissing her cheeks. Then Leo's sister shoved little John into her arms and ran off to shoo another child away from the water. That one small and natural act of being handed a child without being asked made Maggie feel like she was part of the family. She looked down at the toddler, who was oblivious to how dirty he was from playing all day, and hugged his little body into her. Nudging her nose under his chin, he began to giggle as she tickled him.

When she looked up, Leo was staring. She nodded and smiled back at him, then followed him up the path while he carried their heavy luggage. This time, when they entered the kitchen, Maggie felt like she was home. She walked over to the stove and lifted the lid to see what was cooking. She halfway expected Rosa to pop her with her wooden spoon and realized that she wouldn't care if she had, because that's what families do.

They had a "welcome home" feast that night. Rosa invited both Father G and Patty. However, when Patty showed up, she had brought a plus one. Rosa eyed Patty warily but was happy to host Stefano. Rosa kept Stefano occupied in conversation about the farm's award-winning purple artichokes and the honey Stefano's bees made from the flowers.

When Patty walked to refill her wine, Maggie snuck up beside her, "So, how's the beekeeper keeping?"

Patty smirked while she took a sip of her wine, then answered, "Tell me about the gondolier chasing you to the States and bringing you back with an engagement ring on your finger."

"Touche!" Maggie answered. "But all kidding aside, you look happy."

Patty pulled her in for a big hug. "I am. And I can see that you are, too."

After all of the dishes were cleared, the group fell comfortably into a conversation. The children had become bored with the adult chit-chat and had escaped upstairs. When there was a lull in the discussion, Father G motioned to Rosa. "Leo, I need to tell you something. Michael came out to Sant' Erasmus two nights ago."

Leo shot out of his chair, knocking it over on the floor. "I hope you told him to go to hell."

Father G moved to Leo's side of the table, picked up the chair, and eased Leo back into it. "Your mom reacted similarly, but thankfully she let Michael apologize. And after much prayer, she came to talk to me. She was worried about how you would react. Please hear her out."

Leo took a deep breath. "Sorry, Mama."

Rosa nodded to acknowledge him. "Michael came to ask the family for forgiveness. It was hard for him to tell me everything, but it was even harder to hear. Thankfully, we already knew most of what Michael had to say from Mr. Bianco. God bless that man. Michael was ashamed of his lie and the turmoil it caused. He didn't try to push it off on his mom. He completely blamed himself for not being a stronger man. He said he would not blame us if we never forgave him, but he hoped one day we would. He also said he and his father would love the opportunity to reunite our family. I told him I appreciated his honesty and would pass the message on to the rest of the family. Then, he hugged me and left."

Stefano sat beside her, and he patted her hand. She sighed, shaking her head, and Leo thought she had come to the end of her story, but she continued. "I know his lie affected you more than anyone, but I ask you to try and forgive him. I believe once you do, you will finally have the peace you have been searching for."

Father G placed his hand on Leo's shoulder, "Your mama is correct. Forgiveness is not excusing the harm done to you, but it does bring the peace that helps you go on with life."

"I hear you, and I'm grateful to both of you for trying to help me through this. I'm not ready to forgive him yet. I'll pray that Jesus will open my heart." Leo knew they were both right, but he couldn't let go of his anger. He worried what might happen the next time he ran into Michael. He felt Maggie lean into him as she whispered in his ear, "I love you, Leo." And for her, he was most grateful.

43

NEW BEGINNINGS

Stefano walked Patty home from dinner. As they approached her front porch, she noticed the door was slightly ajar. People left their doors open on the island, so it wasn't concerning. Still, she distinctly remembered pulling it closed against the wind.

He noticed the concern on her face. "Can I come in for a minute? I want to make sure you're safe."

The island was the safest place she knew. Still, something didn't feel right, so she agreed. She gasped when she walked inside. Her shelves had been knocked over, and things were strewn across the room. "Why?" she cried out. "Why would anyone ransack a flower shop?" Then her mind went back to the lady that had come to her shop that morning asking for a mandrake plant.

Patty ran out the back door and into the greenhouse. When she focused on the hanging yellow tape encircling the mandrake plants, she knew the culprit. "Everything is perfect here. They must have been after the cash in my till," she yelled out, knowing there wasn't a penny in the cash register.

"Well, they're gone now. Are you going to be okay? I can stay here if you're frightened."

She smiled into his eyes. No one had worried about her since Brett had passed, and it made her heart soar. "I'll be fine. Probably just some teenagers." But she knew it wasn't teenagers. It was the woman who came into her shop periodically, the tall Venetian.

PATTY STEEPED a cup of tea and took it to her favorite seagrass chair that sat in the keeping room. Propping her feet on its ottoman, she replayed the odd interaction with the dark-haired woman.

She had found her on the front porch an hour before her store opened, examining the ornamental mandrakes. She didn't look up when she heard Patty open the door. Her age was hard to pinpoint but she was probably in her mid-50s. She was wearing a fitted red coat with matching leather gloves.

She tore off one of the plant's leaves without acknowledging Patty and waved it quickly under her nose. That small act made Patty realize that the woman was more than just a friendly visitor.

"We don't open for another hour. Can I help you with something?"

The woman tossed the plant's leaf onto the porch and slowly fixed her gaze onto Patty's face. "I heard that you sold mandrake plants. I've come to see for myself. The idiot that told me obviously doesn't know the difference between a true mandrake and a lookalike." She paused and looked deep into Patty's eyes. Patty pulled back under the intensity of her stare as a smirk slowly played upon the woman's face. "Are you the one they call the foreign witch?" she spit out with disgust.

Patty looked away from the intensity of the woman's gaze. She tried to re-focus on the woman's face but never got past the beauty mark beside her left eye. Trying to steady her voice, she answered, "Yes, but people are mistaken."

"Obviously," she spit out in a small laugh. Giving Patty another once over, she turned her attention back to the plant. "Are these the only mandrakes you have?" she asked. When Patty paused, their eyes locked once again.

Patty recoiled from her stare. "Yes, they are my treasures." The woman narrowed her eyes on Patty. *She knows I'm lying*, Patty thought but stuck to her story. The woman spun around on her three-inch stilettos and walked away down the drive.

A cold shiver ran up Patty's spine. She held the mug of tea tightly with both hands, begging for its warmth. The woman had breezed in and out of her shop many times before, but they had never conversed. She was always accompanied by a shorter, more homely woman who handled all of the transactions and mainly bought herbs and seeds. This time, she came alone.

A sense of doom climbed her spine as she wondered how the Venetian woman knew that she had mandrakes. As she pondered this, she laughed. The whole island knows about the mandrakes; Father G told everyone at Mass. But the one person that mattered to Patty was Stefano, and he hadn't asked about them.

Her thoughts drifted to Stefano. She had lied to him about only having native plants in her garden all of those years. If only one bee had gotten into her greenhouse and back out to the colony, it could have poisoned the whole colony. She had read bees usually aren't drawn to poisonous plants like azaleas. But the mandrake had a tempting blue flower that had tricked human beings much more intelligent than a bee. She knew what she had to do — destroy the mandrakes.

44

HELP

Patty knew that she had been poisoned. The toxins coursed through her veins, leaving her disoriented and confused. Fumbling, she grabbed her phone. She had to call someone for help, but who? Stefano didn't carry around a cell phone. Suddenly, Maggie's face popped into her mind. She hurriedly scanned her contacts as her hands began to shake.

"Hold it together," she told herself. "Just a bit longer. I've got to get help." Blinking hard, trying to clear her focus, she stared into the phone. "Just type. Hurry before it's too late." She struggled to take a deep breath as the buzzing in her ears became piercing. She was about to pass out. "There it is, US-Maggie," and their last conversation jumped to the screen. Her fingers were tingling and numb. She typed two words: "HELP MANDRAKES."

Maggie walked out her bedroom door heading down for breakfast, but the ding of her phone made her stop. She almost shrugged it off, but something made her turn back.

Then she saw Patty's message and knew her happy morning had just changed.

P ATTY HEARD the beeping of machines and the scuttle of people around her. She tried and tried to open her eyes, but they were too heavy. She would rest a little more. The next time she heard voices, she tried a little harder. She felt a warm hand holding hers. Brett. Brett was here. But as soon as she remembered him, she felt the familiar pain in her heart. It couldn't be Brett; he was gone. Her heart ached as she wondered what would happen if she just stayed asleep. Could she be with Brett?

Then she felt the warmth of the large, strong hand again. Who was holding her hand? She remembered...Stefano. She oriented herself to Sant' Erasmus. She pictured her island, then her house, then the Venetian woman. Her anger gave her strength, and her eyes popped open. She blinked several times, trying to clear the blur. The many doctors surrounding her bed were talking to the person holding her hand. The beekeeper.

All at once, everyone in the room noticed she was awake and quickly turned their attention to Patty. Stefano jumped to his feet to get closer. *"Ciao, bella,"* he said and kissed her on the forehead. Patty tried to talk, but her brain worked faster than her mouth. She squeezed Stefano's hand and said, "Someone. Took. Mandrake."

The doctor moved in closer. "Try to stay calm. Every-thing will be alright." He turned to one of the other doctors and told them to call the police, then turned his attention back to Patty. "You're still very sick, Ms. Patty. We are calling the police, but we need you to stay calm as your body heals. I don't need to tell you this, but your body is fighting the effects of poison. Thank God we know what poisoned you since you collapsed beside the plant. We treated you quickly, but your organs are still healing. It may be a couple of weeks. You should be back to normal in time."

Patty only nodded. The weight of her eyelids was more than she could fight, and she fell back to sleep almost immediately. The next time she woke up, it was dark. The only sounds were the beep of machines and a gentle snore. She looked down to see Stefano leaning on the bed, still holding her hand. He felt her movement and popped straight up. Smiling, he pushed a strand of her unruly red hair back from her face. She smiled back and spoke from her heart. "I'm so sorry that I didn't tell you about the mandrakes. I was afraid but knew I had to destroy them. I should have asked for help instead of hiding my mistake. Will you forgive me?"

He rubbed his hand down the side of her face. "I definitely will forgive you, but only if you follow the doctor's orders to heal. We just found each other; I don't want to lose you."

She patted his hand, "I promise. I'll behave. Can you tell me what happened?"

Stefano filled her in on the last five days. "Maggie received your text and called for help. Leo performed CPR until the water ambulance arrived and rushed you to the hospital in Venice. The doctors immediately started dialysis on you, but your body had endured severe poisoning. It's going to take you a few more days to start feeling better."

Patty pulled Stefano in and gently kissed his lips. "Thank

you for caring for me," she said in a whisper. Then she added with a smile, "I'm starving."

Once the police heard that Patty was awake and alert, they came to get information from her. They told her others had come to the hospital with the same toxicology report as hers, but she was the only one who had lived. She explained to them that the mandrake plant could be used for several cures if handled by a professional in a lab. But, it could also be used as a poison in the hands of someone who knew its toxicity.

The police gave Patty a laptop and had her look through a file that held pictures of anyone with a criminal record. She didn't recognize anyone as she flipped through the pages. She had been searching for the Venetian woman and turned the pages quickly. The police picked up on this. "Are you looking for someone in particular?" they asked. She told them about the woman who had visited her and the small beauty mark beside her left eye.

Everyone turned when Stefano cleared his throat loudly. "That same woman has been coming to the island for years. The locals say that she makes one stop then leaves. The stop is with me. She buys my beeswax."

MONICA RECEIVED a text from one of her many pursuers, the Carabinieri. The message said, "You've been set-up. You are being accused of something you didn't do. I know this, because you were in my bed at the time. You can hide out at my place if you'd like."

Monica thought back to the night two weeks prior. It was

March 10. She wondered what she was being accused of doing. "Who would want to frame me?" she mumbled. But then she thought of the string of wives who would fight for the chance to get rid of her.

Pietro and Michael were walking out the front door as Monica approached. She quickly ducked into the doorway of the general store and watched them pass. "This will give me free rein in the house for a bit," she thought. She went to the bedroom and began to throw clothes into a bag when she noticed the partially open bedside drawer. She pulled out a manilla envelope and dumped its contents on the bed. Pictures. Someone had been following her and had several photos of her with other men. She angrily pulled them in for a closer look. Her marriage was over; there was no doubt about that. But who would have followed her? She threw the photos down and picked up a small ledger book. The pages held dates, times, and names of meetings, beginning thirty years ago and running until this week. She recognized several of the names, but the one thing that got her attention was the date March 10th, circled in red.

45

GRAND OPENING

Maggie and Leo bobbed in the water of the canal, waiting for the "Blessing of the Fleet." Leo had brought the idea back to Venice and had asked Father G to bless the kayaks the morning of the grand opening. Now a partner, Mr. Bianco asked if his boats could also be blessed. Numerous vessels were waiting in line behind Venice Adventure Kayaks.

Several boat owners had heard that a priest would be standing on the bridge, sprinkling the boats with holy water. The canal was packed. When Leo looked back, he noticed Pietro sitting in his gondola with Michael in the middle seat. They made eye contact, and Michael nodded at Leo.

Maggie watched their interaction, trying to read the look on Leo's face. "Do you know that man?" she asked. Leo only nodded, so she continued. "I know him, too. His name's Michael." As soon as she spoke, she remembered the name from the night before at dinner. Michael was the man who had tarnished his father's good name.

Leo looked at her with confusion. "How would you know Michael?"

She told Leo the story of Michael in the bar and how he had so many questions about Leo. She shared how she had put the shoe on the other foot to make Michael realize how much losing a father, and having his name smeared, had hurt Leo's family.

Leo slowly began to put the pieces together and realized why Michael had finally told the truth. Something that Maggie had said to Michael must have made him come clean. She had a way of doing that, getting under your skin until you break. A small smile played across his face. She had done that to him, too, but in a very different way.

Leo's smile had confused Maggie, and the look on his face was unreadable. She finally asked, "What? What's so funny?"

"You are. You've changed so many lives in your short time in Venice. It's scary to think what you could do if you lived here forever."

She smiled back at him. "I've got an ever-growing list of changes in my mind. Are there any jet skis in Venice?" she asked with a wink.

They traveled the short distance down the canal, each boat being blessed as they passed under the bridge. Once at their base, the boats bobbed around in the water while Father G gave the final blessing to the VAK building.

Monica stood in the shadows between two buildings across the canal. She watched in disgust at the procession of boats. *They are all fools*, she thought. But then she saw Michael sitting in the gondola with Pietro. Her heart gave a slight glint of sorrow. After all, Michael was her own flesh and blood, and she would miss him in her own way. But she had to leave, at least for the time being.

She scanned the crowd, and her eyes landed on Mita. What was she doing here? All of a sudden, things became clear. Mita's constant obsession with her family, the scrapbook with all of their accolades, and finally, the handwriting from the ledger. Mita had set her up. Her hands balled up tight in a fist. "Sweet little Mita. You will pay, cousin. Not now, but soon," she muttered.

Glancing one last time at Michael, she spun on her heels to leave. "*Arriverderci*," she said over her shoulder and walked toward the second half of her life, away from Venice.

THE MORNING CEREMONY was only the beginning of the celebration. Maggie and Leo spent the day giving tours of the facility and taking reservations for the upcoming year. Their calendar was booked through September, with many online reservations on a waiting list. The grand opening party was scheduled for that evening.

Lights were strung in the garden giving it a festive feel. People wandered throughout the house and garden and spilled into the piazza on the inland side of the business. Davide had sent personal invitations, but there was an open guest list for anyone interested in coming. Everyone that Maggie had met in Venice was there.

Leo called the group out into the garden, stood on the stones of the fountain, and began his welcome speech. "I would like to thank everyone who has come to this happy event; my family, especially my brother Davide, who has decided to help me with this venture; and Mr. Bianco, who believes in me and the purpose of Venice Adventure Kayaks. I would especially like to thank my dad, God rest his soul, who instilled in me the love of the waters in Venice. They must be both treasured and respected." He took a breath and scanned the crowd, made eye contact with Maggie, and held it. "Most of all, I want to thank Maggie, who was able to reset my compass and find my passion in life. But most of all, I want to thank Maggie for saying yes to marrying me. Our biggest adventure is yet to come."

Everyone around began to cheer as Maggie wiped the tears running down her face. Leo's mom and sisters wrapped her up in hugs while Katerina excitedly waited her turn to hug Maggie's neck. As Maggie looked around the crowd, she realized that she felt as comfortable in Venice with these wonderful people surrounding her as she did in Savannah. That thought reassured her of her and Leo's future.

Mr. Bianco then called everyone's attention and offered a toast, "To Venice Adventure Kayaks and the enlightening gift they will be for our city." The crowd held up their drinks, "*Salute!*" Then Mr. Bianco surprised Leo. "To Claudio Vianello, who gave his life as a true hero. And to his loved ones. Let every vessel that passes this plaque hanging on the canal remember him." Mr. Bianco held up a golden plaque with an engraved image of Claudio. Under the picture was the Bible passage from John 15:13, "No greater love is there than to lay down one's life for another." The crowd responded a second time, "*Salute!*"

As the crowd began to scatter, Leo pulled Maggie off alone. They walked to the top of the small bridge that Father G had stood on just that morning. They both peered down into the water, looking at their reflection against the pink sky above. Leo turned and lifted her chin towards him. Just as their lips were about to touch, the sound of something breaking the water's surface caught their attention; a dolphin. Leo looked down at the dolphin curiously and smiled. It was a dolphin that had led Leo to Savannah, and it was a dolphin that was leading them into their future. Bowing his head, he said, "Thank you, my friend."

Peering down the length of the canal, Maggie sighed as she watched the dolphin disappear into the last of the daylight, heading out to the lagoon. Leo wrapped his arms around her as they enjoyed the breathtaking view. She was flooded with emotion, thinking of all that had taken place in the past year. A satisfied smile spread across her face knowing that from then on, whether in Savannah or Venice, all of her future sunsets would take place in the arms of the Savannah Gondolier.

THE END

EPILOGUE

Trevor made his way into the mouth of the channel. It had been a long emotional week; burying his father had affected him in ways he could never have imagined. He was happy he and his dad had made amends and that he had been able to spend most days at the hospital with him.

He was still confused by what his father had told him. "Make things right. The people need to be released from Lazaretto. I didn't have the guts, but you are stronger than me," he had said. *What did that even mean? Did morphine make people talk that crazy?*

Trevor fought back his emotions as he passed the lighthouse. That's when he heard the sounds once again. He began noticing the static noise when he returned to work after the funeral. He tried rubbing his ears, but the sound remained. He would schedule an appointment with an ENT when he got off the ship.

As the ship came to the turn to Lazaretto Creek, he began to hear actual voices, whispers, really. He checked his cell phone to see if a video was playing, then he checked the radio. Both were off. Closing his eyes, he listened more intently and was surprised when an image came to his mind: Maggie. She was surrounded by faceless shapes. She was smiling and seemed happy and protected, but he was outside the group. He rubbed his eyes and thought about his father's words, "The people need to be released from Lazaretto."

"Oh shit! I'm being haunted; the tales are true. Why didn't you tell me, Dad?" he said to himself. How did Maggie fit into all of this? He must find her. She was the only person who could help him. He must get to Maggie.

ACKNOWLEDGEMENTS

This book has brought back memories of growing up on the many waterways of the Low Country. My dad worked very hard from 8-5, but in the afternoons and on weekends, he was 100% available to his family. He taught me how to fish, run a boat, drag for shrimp in the river, and throw a cast net. Thank you, Dad, for sharing your love of the Savannah waterways with me, your river rat. Thank you, Mom, for sharing your ability to cook our catch.

I also want to thank our United States River Pilots. These men work a dangerous job to make our commerce thrive. I have watched firsthand as they jump from a moving pilot boat onto a ship in the absolute worst weather at all hours of the night. Thank you for being so dedicated. I also want to acknowledge the wives and mothers who pray for them every day when they're away. I understand you because I'm one of you. The Saint Erasmus prayer works, trust me.

A huge thank you goes out to my sweet college roommate, who changed around her schedule to go with me to

Italy. I know my work trips are demanding, but I appreciate the sacrifice. I can't wait for our next research adventure and hope that our third roommate and my daughter can accompany us.

Many hands and eyes go into the finished product of this small book. Thank you to my sister, Shannon, for her many reads and constant support; critique partner, Meggie Daly; editor, Patrice MacArthur; cover designer, Sarah Hansen with Okay Creations; cover photographer, Bailey Davidson; and my advanced readers. God has blessed me with many talented individuals, and I am most grateful for your hard work.

The biggest thank you goes to my family, for the unconditional love and support from all of those who call me Mom (and Mayme). My heart is full.

I've saved the best for last. To my husband, John. I know you had no idea of what you were getting into thirty-something years ago, but I thank you for always loving and encouraging me in everything that I do. As I've said many times, our life together is the best adventure I could ever imagine.

ALSO IN THE SAINTS OF SAVANNAH SERIES

THE BLESSING OF THE CELTIC CURSE

The land of her forefathers summons Kathleen Kenny to Ireland. But why now, only weeks before her big wedding? If only her fiancé, Jack, understood that she must go to search for answers. Kathleen is thrust into the culture of "small-town" Ireland as she steps into the McMillon family's world. Handsome Quinn McMillon has recently inherited his father's farm but isn't quite ready to settle down. While Kathleen digs into the lives of her ancestors, her life and that of the townsfolk of Knock become intimately bound in unimaginable ways. Experience the beauty of Savannah, the charm of Ireland, and the shenanigans of a host of unforgettable characters with a feel-good story that's full of surprises until the very last page.

The Blessing of the Celtic Curse

CPSIA information can be obtained
at www.ICGtesting.com
Printed in the USA
LVHW100004210622
721682LV00004B/305